The Tea Shop by the Sea

De-ann Black

Paperback edition published 2021

The Tea Shop by the Sea

ISBN: 9798713896911

Also by De-ann Black (Romance, Action/Thrillers & Children's books). See her Amazon Author page or website for further details about her books, screenplays, illustrations, art and fabric designs.

www.De-annBlack.com

Romance:

The Bookshop by the Seaside
The Sewing Bee
The Quilting Bee
Snow Bells Wedding
Snow Bells Christmas
Summer Sewing Bee
The Chocolatier's Cottage
Christmas Cake Chateau
The Beemaster's Cottage
The Sewing Bee By The Sea
The Flower Hunter's Cottage
The Christmas Knitting Bee
The Sewing Bee & Afternoon Tea
The Vintage Sewing & Knitting Bee
Shed In The City
The Bakery By The Seaside
Champagne Chic Lemonade Money
The Christmas Chocolatier
The Christmas Tea Shop & Bakery
The Vintage Tea Dress Shop In Summer
Oops! I'm The Paparazzi
The Bitch-Proof Suit
The Tea Dress Shop At Christmas

Action/Thrillers: Love Him Forever. Someone Worse. Electric Shadows. The Strife Of Riley. Shadows Of Murder.

Children's books: Faeriefied. Secondhand Spooks. Poison-Wynd. Wormhole Wynd. Science Fashion. School For Aliens.

Colouring books:
Summer Garden. Spring Garden. Autumn Garden. Sea Dream. Festive Christmas. Christmas Garden. Flower Bee. Wild Garden. Faerie Garden Spring. Flower Hunter. Stargazer Space. Bee Garden.

Contents

CHAPTER ONE

Eila arranged the dresses in the window of her shop beside the sea in Scotland. The shelves were stocked with rolls of fabric and she offered a selection of thread and haberdashery items.

Excitement and trepidation flittered through her. She'd taken on the lease of the shop recently and this was her first day opening. The sun was barely up, but she'd been anxious to ensure that everything looked great. She'd been sewing one of the dresses the previous night, and the classic tea dress was now in the window display.

Eila loved sewing and she loved the sea. Living in the city all her thirty–one years, she'd recently been working from her home in Glasgow, building up a little dressmaking business, advertising her creations on her website along with selling fabric and other items that helped make her a profit.

The cost of the lease was less than the rent she paid for her city flat. The online sales of her dresses and fabric gave her the freedom to live anywhere, within reason. So, she'd decided to leave the city and set up shop in a small community on the West Coast of the Scottish Highlands.

The past two weeks had been a blur of activity, working all hours, locked safely away in the little shop that included cottage–style accommodation tucked at the back of the property. It was cosy, nothing grand, but made her feel that life could be better here by the sea, away from her past that had dragged her down bit by bit for so long that she'd barely realised the depths she'd been accustomed to. The sales of her dresses online gave her a glimmer of hope, that she could make her own way in the world — and leave broken relationships with past boyfriends and her broken heart behind her.

She gazed out at the sea, wondering if the man who owned the tea shop nearby would go swimming, like he did every morning. The summer was still warm and the sea looked refreshing. Although she hadn't been deliberately watching him, she'd noticed him while sitting in her shop, sewing away, and wondered why he intrigued her. He looked fit, but there was something about his daily dips that made her want to gaze at him. Perhaps she'd been working too hard and needed a pleasant distraction. She'd heard his name was Gordon, but she'd kept herself to herself while settling into the life here. There was a woman in the grocery shop, Minnie, who'd asked her all sorts of prying questions, offered snippets of local gossip, and invited her to the local quilting bee nights that were held in the function room at the back of Gordon's tea shop.

She'd politely avoided answering the questions, ignored the gossip and promised she'd pop along to the quilting bee when she was ready. She was so busy.

It was a promise she intended keeping. Not yet though, not yet.

Early morning sunlight glistened across the beautiful blue sea in the bay, tempting Gordon to go for his daily swim. First, he had to finish baking the cakes for the tea shop he owned. The air was filled with the delicious aroma of vanilla and chocolate and mingled with the scent of the sea wafting in the front door. The warm breeze merited being allowed in as summertime lingered in the little village on the coast.

The tea shop nestled in a row of quaint shops at the edge of the harbour and had a lovely view of the coastline. The shops were bordered by a patchwork of fields and tree covered hills. Cottages and farmhouses were tucked into the greenery.

The windows of the tea shop glinted in the sunshine and flowers cascaded from the hanging baskets outside the entrance.

Inside, Gordon had opted for a traditional look for his tea shop, retaining most of the original decor, vintage glass lamps and the fireplace. His cakes ranged from old–fashioned favourites to fancy new recipes he loved to experiment with. As well as cakes, his menu had a selection of scones, fruit filled tarts and savoury treats. He'd created his own confectionery range with delicious sweets including chocolates, butterscotch, truffles, fudge and Scottish tablet.

At barely eight o'clock in the morning there was little chance of any customers wandering into the tea shop, not that he would've minded. The small community didn't stand on ceremony, and the friendships he'd built locally were the closest to family he could've wished for. Like most families, they were a mixed bag of characters, but setting up his tea shop here was the best move he'd ever made. Single and in his thirties, he still hoped to meet someone to settle down with and raise a family of his own. Maybe this summer the woman who was meant for him would walk into his life. And if not?

Well, he was happy with his tea shop and the people frequenting it, including the ladies of the quilting bee. Their lively quilting bee nights were held in the function room of the tea shop and the gossip alone was always entertaining.

As the sea air drifting in tempted him to go for the daily dip that kept him lean and strong, he put a spurt on to finish the cakes.

He piped whipped cream over two vanilla sponges, topped them with locally picked brambles and Scottish tayberries, carried them through from the kitchen to the front of the tea shop and placed them in the chilled display cabinet.

Adjusting the sponges so that his butterfly cakes could be seen in the display, he saw Pearl run past the window, a flurry of auburn hair and rosy cheeks. She didn't even glance in. No one appeared to be chasing her, and as she was wearing her gingham apron he doubted she was out for a jog. Not that he'd ever seen Pearl jog. She was one of the quilting bee ladies, in her fifties, and although he expected her work as a local housekeeper kept her fit, he didn't think she was inclined to go for a morning gallop. No, something must be wrong, and if so, there was only one place she was heading. He peered out the door...

Yes, there she was, dashing into Minnie's grocery shop. Some hot gossip was brewing. He was sure of it.

Unable to contain his curiosity, even with the sea beckoning him, he hurried along to Minnie's grocery shop and went inside.

Two customers, Euan and Judy, were holding fresh morning rolls, bread, butter and other items, engrossed in whatever news Pearl was revealing to Minnie. The grocery shop was the local gossip hub and Minnie was never insulted when accused of being a gossipmonger. She was, and that was all there was to it.

Euan, a tall, strapping farmer in his thirties, who lived nearby, glanced at Gordon as if something horrendous had happened. Judy, co–owner with her husband, Jock, of the bar restaurant next door to the tea shop, gripped tight to her plain loaf and jar of strawberry jam. She pursed her lips in obvious disapproval of the news.

Minnie was in her fifties and wore her brown hair pinned up in a tidy bun. She looked at Gordon as he walked in. 'You'll never guess who is coming back here.'

Gordon reckoned she was right. He hadn't a clue. His blank expression confirmed this.

Minnie took a deep breath and let rip with the announcement. 'Sholto and his two sons are coming back to live here for a whole month!'

This meant nothing to Gordon.

'And he's bringing Cairn with him,' Minnie added, sounding snippy.

Pearl spoke up, joining the dots for Gordon. 'Sholto is extremely wealthy, made of money. He owns the biggest house in this area. The one hidden high up, surrounded by trees. It would have a view of the sea if he allowed it, but he doesn't. Privacy and snobbery are rife with that man.'

Gordon frowned. 'I thought that house was all closed and shuttered.'

Minnie nodded firmly. 'It is, and has been for years. A lovely big house abandoned by a man who lives in Edinburgh. He owns a very successful menswear and tailoring company. Owns the building where their offices are in the city. He runs it with his two sons, Hamish and Fraser. Cairn is Sholto's assistant. Those three are all about the same age as you and Euan. Pearl is paid to look after the house here, and one of the local men checks the maintenance of it.'

'Did Sholto contact you?' Euan asked Pearl.

'I got a message from his office saying — get the house ready. Sholto is coming back this weekend and bringing his sons and Cairn with him.' Pearl ran a distraught hand through her hair. 'I'll have to pull the dust sheets off the furniture and clean it from top to toe. Sholto is very fussy. He pays well, and I've had a chunk of money paid into my bank, but that's not going to buy me the time I need to get that house fit for them arriving.'

'Don't worry,' Minnie assured her. 'We'll rally the quilting bee ladies and all muck in.'

'Thank you, Minnie.' Pearl seemed genuinely relieved. 'My stomach flipped when I got the message this morning that they were coming back.'

'Are they difficult men to deal with?' Gordon tried to sound tactful.

Minnie adjusted her spectacles that were threatening to steam up with rage. 'Difficult? That's putting it nicely.'

'They don't even belong here anymore,' Judy objected. 'They live and work in Edinburgh. Sholto should've sold the house years ago to someone who would actually live in it.'

Pearl sighed reluctantly. 'The house is part of Sholto's heritage, where he grew up, where he'd built his tailoring business from scratch. It's been in his family for years.'

A lull fell over the shop as this was considered.

'Even so,' Minnie said grudgingly, 'Sholto should've handled things better instead of waltzing off to Edinburgh. Him and those handsome sons of his are nothing but trouble. You mark my words. We were all looking forward to a long, relaxing summer and the promise of a warm September. A nice long summer was just what we were due. And now Sholto comes barging in with his money and power to spoil everything.'

'So he'll upset the equilibrium? Is that what you're upset about?' Gordon asked.

'Yes, and the trouble they'll cause.' Minnie shook her head in dismay.

'You said they were handsome?' Gordon wondered if this was an issue.

Pearl fixed Gordon with an incredulous look. 'Huh! You and Euan are fine looking men, handsome yourselves. But wait until you see these men. They're in a whole different league.'

'Heartbreakers,' said Judy. 'All of them — including Cairn.'

'Especially Cairn,' Minnie emphasised. 'He's a cold–hearted charmer if ever I met one. All blond hair and gorgeous blue eyes, chiselled features and a ruthless romantic.'

Gordon wasn't sure what that was exactly, but it didn't sound endearing.

'I love my husband dearly,' Judy confessed, 'but even I felt my heart flutter when I was around Cairn, or Hamish or Fraser.' She sighed, disappointed in herself. 'Or Sholto himself.'

Pearl nodded in agreement with Judy. 'These men are the business equivalent of Hollywood heartthrobs. They cause the women to...well, not misbehave, but at least to think about doing it.'

'Why are they coming here?' Gordon wanted to know.

'That's the big question and we don't have the answer,' explained Pearl. 'I wasn't told, and that means it's none of my business.'

‘Which ultimately means it’s all of our business,’ Minnie snipped.

‘I’ll find out everything I can,’ Pearl promised. ‘But I’ll have to get a shifty on with clearing the dust sheets and cleaning the house. And what about the garden? It needs done.’

‘I’ll help with that.’ Euan was quick to volunteer.

Pearl smiled her thanks to him.

Gordon chimed–in. ‘What can I do to help?’

‘Keep steady, stay strong and back us ladies up,’ Minnie told him. ‘And keep a regular supply of cakes on hand in case of emotional emergencies. We’ll use the tea shop as our meeting hub as well as for the quilting bee, if that’s okay with you, Gordon?’

‘Yes, of course. Anything to help,’ he assured them.

A message came through on Pearl’s phone. She read it and then stared at Minnie and the others.

‘What?’ Minnie asked, concerned what the message had relayed.

‘I asked a friend who works for them in Edinburgh if she knew why Sholto was coming back here,’ Pearl explained. ‘Apparently, Sholto wants to come home so they can think up new ideas for their tailoring designs, come back to the source of where it all started. He hasn’t told his sons or Cairn yet. He’s having a meeting this morning to tell them they have to pack their bags and head here.’

Minnie looked wide–eyed. ‘Can you imagine how well that will go down with them?’

Pearl winced and shook her head.

Gordon didn’t know these men, but even he felt the trepidation of what was brewing in Edinburgh...

Four of the most handsome and well–dressed men in the city were arguing in one room.

The third floor boardroom had a view of the Edinburgh streets. Sunlight glinted off the buildings and a heat haze indicated that the day was going to be a scorcher — but it was no match for the temperature at the meeting as tempers flared.

‘Give me one reason why we shouldn’t go back home for a while,’ Sholto demanded. As head of the family business, and owner of the bespoke tailoring company from the ground floor to the boardroom, he was losing patience with one of his three sons. Hamish, thirty–three, rarely argued with his father. Sholto and

Hamish shared the same taste in classic tailoring. They agreed on most things. Hamish's younger brother, Fraser, thirty–one, had his own ideas about the bespoke tailoring business. A family business started by Sholto and shared by his sons.

At fifty–none of anyone's business, Sholto defied his age. His assistant, Cairn, at thirty–five looked slightly younger than Hamish. They were a formidable four–man team. It took a lot to shake the foundations Sholto had so carefully built. Recent ructions had caused tremors and a slight downturn in profits. The meeting was called to discuss how to breathe new ideas into the traditionally built company. This included leaving Edinburgh for a working holiday on the West Coast of the Highlands.

'I have no objections to rethinking the business, but heading over to the West Coast wouldn't be my plan. I'd focus on better advertising and marketing,' said Hamish.

'Advertising is part of the marketing mix,' Fraser chipped–in.

Sholto shot Fraser a look not to rub against the grain of Hamish's immaculate wool suit.

'I don't see why we have to leave Edinburgh. This is where we create our designs. I see no benefit in packing our bags and going on a working break all the way over there,' Hamish complained.

Sholto stood firm. 'Our marketing campaigns haven't boosted sales sufficiently during the past few seasons. We're stuck in a rut in the city, seeing the same things we always see, doing the same things. We're not creating anything new that's sparking with our customers.'

'Neither have our main rivals,' Fraser added.

Another shot was fired at Fraser from Sholto's piercing grey eyes.

'There has to be a more productive way to deal with a slump. Though we're not exactly in a downturn. We're ticking over quite nicely,' Hamish argued. 'Things could pick up for our winter collection.'

'I don't think it's outstanding enough,' Sholto told him.

Hamish shook his head. 'Nothing is ever enough for you.'

'The standards I have set for this company have made us a success, and I plan to continue raising the bar,' Sholto snapped at Hamish.

'Our spring collection didn't do too badly,' said Hamish.

Sholto stared right through him. 'It was bland.'

There was a furious rustling of papers as Hamish searched for the information in his bulging folder of paperwork to counter Sholto's argument. 'It says here that our new shirt and tie collection faired well, equalling last year's sales.' He found a printout of their profits on their suits. 'According to this there's equal interest being shown in our tailoring abilities.'

'Equalling and not bettering our sales is a slippery slope in the tailoring design part of our business.' Sholto sounded defiant.

'I think you're overreacting, as always,' Hamish said to him.

'That's preposterous,' said Sholto.

Hamish agreed, but he wasn't willing to withdraw on his bluster. 'You sound just like mother.' His bronze hair, as he preferred to call it, rather than sandy red, was backlit by the sun streaming through the boardroom window, making him look like he'd just stepped through the fires of hell, which in a way he had. He couldn't have issued a worse insult to his father. Comparing Sholto to his ex–wife was the ultimate in low blows. Cynthia owned a successful cookery school a safe distance from them. Their paths rarely crossed, but their verbal swords did on the few occasions correspondence was required to sort out family monetary matters. Sometimes Sholto won. Sometimes Cynthia. A huge achievement on Cynthia's part as few challenged Sholto and emerged with their souls intact.

Cynthia had never forgiven her sons for choosing the tailoring side of the business with their father. She'd hoped at least one son would've opted to train as a master chef, an expert in patisserie, something her school excelled at. She'd thought Fraser, her favourite, would've used his knack for baking to become a master at his craft. But no. Sholto got them. The two sons stood shoulder to shoulder with daddy.

Her marriage to Sholto had been a long and arduous one. Even Hamish wondered if his mother had deliberately let herself get caught naked and dripping with white icing with a sexy patisserie chef from Paris who was over to instruct one of her classes on the art of wedding cake sugarcraft. Sholto was the one who found them. Forgiveness was off the agenda. Divorce was swift. Whatever the chef had been doing with the icing spatula to Cynthia was never openly discussed again at the dinner table. They rarely mentioned her. A low blow indeed from Hamish to cast her into the ring during the morning's disagreement.

Cairn's ice blue eyes flicked from Sholto to Hamish. Which one would exit the arena first? Cairn's money was on Hamish.

The sun brought no hint of warmth to Cairn's features and sexy blond hair. His sharp nose and chiselled cheekbones bore a cold beauty, emphasised by his silky hair swept back from his smooth forehead. Shorter at the sides, his hair was the most noticeable of his assets, along with a tall, wiry frame and broad shoulders. They'd used Cairn to advertise a range of suits once when a male model refused to stand in the snow in the Scottish Highlands during a photo shoot for their brochure. Cairn braved the freezing landscape without complaint for over an hour while the photographs were taken. Bare–chested and stripped down to his boxers, he'd changed out of his clothes several times in the biting January wind and worn the suits as required. For someone so manly, Cairn had a beauty about him. Not beauty of the soul, for he was, by his own admission, a nasty character. Loyal but nasty. The perfect man for the job as Sholto's assistant. Sholto didn't suffer fools gladly, and Cairn made sure his employer didn't have to. If Sholto could've had a third son, he would've chosen Cairn.

All of them were over six–feet–tall with lean builds and broad shoulders. They suited wearing suits. They wore them well. Hamish was the strongest and sturdiest of them, akin to Sholto. Fraser was enigmatic and gave an air of vintage handsomeness. Well–cut, light brown hair and grey eyes, along with a clean–cut image, and penchant for three–piece suits with a pocket watch tucked into his waistcoats, made him look like he belonged to a bygone era. Sometimes he wished this was true, especially when arguments erupted. He hated his equilibrium being disturbed but was adept at disturbing others. A fault he had no intention of working on.

There was silence in the boardroom. Seething silence, as only Sholto could create on such a hot day. Even Cairn tugged at the collar of his white shirt. And Cairn was the coolest of them all.

Sholto finally shouted, 'Don't bring your mother into this discussion, Hamish.'

'Yes,' Minnie mused. 'I bet Sholto and his sons are arguing hammer and tongs at the moment. Even ice cold Cairn won't be able to dowse that fiery exchange.'

CHAPTER TWO

Gordon's mind was buzzing from all the gossip discussed in Minnie's grocery shop, but he knew that he had work to do.

'I'd better get back to my tea shop and finish the cakes. Will you still be having your quilting bee this evening?'

Minnie nodded firmly. 'Despite the chaos that Sholto's caused, we won't be missing out on our quilting bee because of him.'

'I'll bake another couple of your favourite chocolate cakes for tonight,' said Gordon.

'That would be great,' Minnie told him.

'It'll give us something extra tasty to look forward to,' Pearl added. 'We'll need it after all the work Sholto's foisted on us.'

'I'll come up and give you a hand to get the house ready,' Judy assured her. 'We'll round up a few of the bee members and have that big house of his sorted in jig time.'

The relief showed again on Pearl's face.

Gordon wished he could help them more, but he couldn't close his tea shop for the day. 'I'll have lots of tasty treats for you all this evening,' he promised, hoping to bolster them.

At the mention of *tasty treats*, Minnie's dog's floppy ears perked up. Bracken had been snuggled in his basket beside the counter. He was a mid–size, mixed breed, with black, white and brown colouring, and loved being lavished with attention from customers.

'Don't mention things like that,' Minnie whispered to Gordon. 'Bracken hasn't had his breakfast yet.'

Gordon smiled, jokingly zipped his mouth, and went to head out.

'Have you spoken yet to our newcomer, Eila?' Minnie called to him.

Gordon halted. 'No, she's been tucked in her dress shop stitching away, I presume.'

'She's been keeping herself to herself,' Minnie commented. 'But she's opening her dress shop today. I saw the notice in her window.'

'I've got my eye on two of the fabric bundles she's selling online.' Pearl sounded enthusiastic. 'Lovely cotton fabric. Ideal for quilting. I'm thinking of popping in and buying them from her.'

'Even though she's been quiet,' Judy began, 'we should try and support her opening day.'

'I'm sure she's got a reason for being on the quiet side,' Euan remarked.

'She's bought groceries in my shop several times and I've gleaned some information from her,' said Minnie. 'She's definitely from Glasgow and says she wanted to move here to have a shop by the sea rather than continue working from her home in the city. But that's about all I've pried from her.'

Gordon lingered at the door, listening to them. He'd glimpsed Eila a few times, but they'd never met.

'Maybe she's shy,' Euan suggested.

Minnie nodded. 'Some city folk aren't used to their business being everybody's business. They're guarded, but she'll soon join in with things. We'll give her a chance to get to know us. I'll invite her again to the quilting bee.'

As they went on to gossip about other things, Gordon left them to it. He had cakes to ice and buttercream to whip up before his dip in the sea.

The air was fresh, and he breathed it in deeply as he walked back to the tea shop.

Eila's dress shop was further along the esplanade and he had no reason to walk past it. He'd wanted to peer in and say hello, but he sensed something about her. From the glimpses of her as she hurried past his tea shop, usually carrying groceries from Minnie's shop, she looked very pleasant. Very attractive. Not that he was thinking of pursuing her. She looked like a young woman with a lot on her mind, and steeped in her own world. He reckoned Minnie was right. She simply needed time to get to know them. Often newcomers were thrown into the deep end once they arrived, barely given a chance to breathe before being swept into the chaos of the local community. Anyone thinking that this was a quiet little seaside bolt hole was mistaken.

Eila walked through from the cottage at the back of the shop where she'd been busy working at her sewing machine. She'd considered setting it up near the counter in the front shop, but she preferred to sew in private. In the evenings she'd been sewing in the cottage, so it made sense not to have to set the machine up in the shop. She had another sewing machine, a lovely vintage model but it didn't work, and planned to put it in the shop to add to the modern vintage style of the decor.

The dresses she designed were classic tea dresses and day dresses that were both comfortable for everyday wear but could be spruced up with accessories for special events. Ideal for parties and yet suitable for all day use such as shopping or strolling along the seashore, something she'd yet to do. Her list of things to do was quite long, but she'd do those once she was settled, and she wasn't settled yet, especially as she wasn't sure of the response to her opening a little dress shop in what appeared to be a tight–knit community.

As she hung another dress in the window display, she glanced out at the shore.

There he was! Swimming in the sea, as if he hadn't a care in the world, and all the time to go with it.

She wondered how he did it. Managing a tea shop was bound to be a full–time business. Even when he was closed he'd be baking cakes and scones and those delicious looking chocolate treats she'd glimpsed in his front windows. Truffles and chocolate fudge by the looks of them. She planned to indulge in a box of those, and one of the fruit filled tarts that were glazed to perfection.

She watched Gordon swim along the shore. He seemed less relaxed than previous days. He was powering through the water. Usually she felt calm just watching him, except for the increased beating of her heart when he'd emerge from the sea and walk back up to the shore in his trunks. It was doubtful that he was intentionally putting on a display. Gordon looked like he was at ease with things, fit looking without the appearance of deliberate training to give him a muscular physique. Gordon's muscles were lean and strong but seemed accrued from hard work and daily swimming.

She added a lovely embroidery thread display to the window. It was a new range of colours with sea blues and soft amber tones that were ideal for the summer and autumn theme embroidery patterns that were available. By the time she'd done this, Gordon had finished his swim and was now striding out of the sea. He picked up his towel from the sand and began drying himself off.

Running his hands through his wet, dark hair, he headed back to his tea shop.

He couldn't see her watching him, for she had stepped back out of view. But he suddenly glanced over at her shop, as if sensing he was being watched, and then continued on.

Gordon went upstairs where he lived above the tea shop, and jumped in the shower to rinse the salt water and sand off. As he showered he wondered if the woman from the dress shop had been watching him. He'd felt like he was being watched. And yet he'd seen no sign of her.

Shrugging the notion away, he stepped out of the shower and got dressed in a clean white shirt and dark trousers ready for the day's work.

Pearl hurried along from the grocery shop, heading home to pick up her cleaning things. She saw Eila in the dress shop window, paused and chapped on the glass, startling her.

'I know you're not open,' Pearl called through to her.

Eila saw a woman with a fresh faced look and rosy cheeks wave in to her. She opened the door. 'I'm opening soon.'

'I'm Pearl. A friend of Minnie's. She owns the grocery shop.'

Eila nodded acknowledgement.

'I'm in a crazy hurry because of...well...it's not really anything that's of issue to you...' Then Pearl reconsidered. 'But, maybe I should tell you, warn you about Sholto, his two sons, and his assistant, coming back to live here for a wee while. Those four men will be here this weekend.'

Eila frowned. 'I'm sorry, but I don't know anyone here, not yet. I've been busy getting my shop ready.'

Pearl nodded, but became distracted by the fabric on sale.

'I want to buy a couple of your fabric bundles. Could you put them aside for me? I've got to get the big house cleaned before Sholto arrives.'

Eila wasn't sure what was going on, but clearly Pearl was in a tizzy. 'I'd be glad to put them aside for you, Pearl. What ones were you interested in?'

'The pansy selection in shades of blue and lavender.'

'I know that one. I'll keep it for you.'

'And the vintage floral fat quarter bundle in spring tones.'

'Okay, I'll put them aside, and you can pick them up later.'

'I don't know if I'll be able to pick them up before you close. It's bedlam today.'

'Pick them up tomorrow if you like.'

'Thank you. And are you coming along to the quilting bee tonight at Gordon's tea shop? The ladies would love to meet you. I know quite a few of them are interested in your dresses and fabric.' Pearl eyed the thread. 'I like your embroidery thread. Are those new summer and autumn colours?'

'They are. I thought they looked lovely.'

'I do like to embroider, and can't resist new thread.'

'I'll try to come along to the quilting bee tonight.'

'You'll be made very welcome.' Pearl smiled. 'But I need to rush. Sholto thinks that money solves everything.'

Leaving Eila wondering what was going on, but surmising that someone named Sholto, presumably with his sons and assistant, was causing Pearl to be flustered.

Eila closed the door again. She hadn't officially opened yet, but she'd had her first sale. And an invitation to the quilting bee.

Eila then saw a man walk past. She'd seen him a few times, but they hadn't acknowledged each other.

Euan nodded in at her as he went by, hazel eyes looking right at her.

She nodded back at him and watched him walk away. He was quite handsome, she thought, strong and capable with untamed burnished gold hair. His clothes were casual but classic, like a gentleman farmer. A man in his thirties with an air of old money. His trousers, waistcoat and jacket were in muted tones of dark green, ochre and bronze, expensive but work–worn. She admired the cut and the colours. If she hadn't preferred dressmaking, she'd have ventured into a career in men's tailoring like her father.

She wondered what the man's name was. No doubt she'd find out later at the quilting bee.

Gordon held the cake in his hands and considered the implications. Should he pop along to Eila's shop and give her the cake for her opening day? If so, what would she think? What if she didn't want any cakes like this cream filled sponge in her shop?

'Planning on doing something with that?' Judy asked, popping her head into his tea shop. She was on her way to the bar restaurant to ask her husband Jock to hold the fort while she helped Pearl.

'I'm not sure. I thought I'd give it to Eila for her shop opening.' He sat it down on a plate.

'You should. It would give you a chance to meet her.'

Gordon swithered. 'But it's a bit presumptuous.'

'No, it's not. Hurry along and hand it in. I'll keep an eye on the tea shop for you.'

Gordon was spurred on by Judy's confidence. 'Okay, I'll be back in a tick.'

There was no one in the dress shop when Gordon walked in. Not even Eila. He heard the whir of a sewing machine coming from the cottage area at the back of the shop.

'Hello?' he called through to her, feeling this was all wrong. Things like this rarely went well for him. Well–meaning meddlers were often unwelcome.

Eila walked through and was startled to see Gordon standing there, fully clothed, offering her a large cake on a lovely vintage floral plate.

'Happy opening day,' he said, wishing he'd rehearsed what he was going to say to her. Seeing her up close affected him. He knew she was pretty from the glimpses of her, but she was truly lovely with beautiful blue eyes that viewed him with curiosity.

'Thank you, Gordon.' She accepted the cake and put it on the counter. 'That was very kind of you.' She swept her shoulder–length blonde hair back and smiled at him.

Hearing her say his name threw him more than her easy acceptance of his cake. He knew her name, so neither of them bothered with formal introductions.

'You own the tea shop?' It was less of a question and more of a statement.

'I do. I heard that you were opening today. Minnie and some other ladies from the quilting bee mentioned it to me.' He felt the need to explain, hoping the inclusion of the ladies didn't make him appear like a creepy stalker, watching her, waiting for the moment she opened her door so he could present her with a cake.

'Minnie and Pearl have both invited me to the quilting bee. I've been so busy, and getting used to things here.'

'Are you coming along tonight?'

'Yes, I'll pop along for a bit. I've never been to a quilting bee before.'

'Are you a quilter?' He glanced at the dresses. 'You're obviously into sewing.'

'I've dabbled, but clothes are what I mainly sew.'

'The ladies sew all sorts of things, including dresses, and they knit and embroider.'

'I'll take along some sewing,' she said, happy that she didn't need to have any quilting skills.

'It's quite a social evening. They do get some sewing done, but there's plenty of chatter, catching up on local news.'

'Gossip?'

'Eh, yes.'

Eila smiled, obviously teasing him.

He smiled back at her. 'Lots of tea and cakes to enjoy too.'

'I'll have a light dinner.'

'I serve suppers in the tea shop on the bee nights, so if you're busy with work and don't have time to cook dinner, come and have something to eat with me.'

She blinked.

'What I mean is, suppers are available in my tea shop.' Calm down, he scolded himself. You sound like a fool.

'That's handy to know.'

She noticed his eyes were blue–green, like the sea, and his tawny hair was lightened from being in the sun. His open neck white shirt looked cool to the touch, but there was an unmistakable warmth in his manner.

They gazed at each other for a moment, and then Gordon said, 'Well, good luck with your new venture. I'd better get back to the tea shop. A busy day ahead, as always. I'm running a bit late today.' Listening to gossip at Minnie's shop had mucked up his schedule.

'Caught up in swimming further out to sea,' she remarked, thinking this was the reason.

She'd seen him swimming! He hadn't realised.

'Not that I was watching you,' she explained. 'I've seen you a few times when I've been working near the window. It's a lovely view of the sea. I'm so used to seeing the city.'

'I try to go for a swim most mornings.'

'I didn't recognise you at first with your clothes on,' she said, then blushed. 'With your eh...working clothes on...not your...swimming trunks.' And nothing else. A towel draped around his shoulders didn't count or the flip flops he wore to walk across the esplanade to the shore.

She wasn't sure which one of them blushed the rosiest.

Desperate to appear unperturbed, she gestured towards the cake. 'It looks delicious. Thank you again for the cake.'

'You're very welcome.' He headed towards the door, feeling like an idiot as he fumbled opening it. 'See you later, if you come along to the quilting bee.' He hurried out.

She waved and sighed. What a thing to say about his lack of clothes! If there was any gossip tonight, her comment to Gordon was sure to be part of it.

Gordon hurried into the tea shop. No one was there yet except Judy. She laughed when she saw him.

'You're looking...flushed. What happened? Did she kiss you to thank you for the cake?' she teased him.

'No, she was very nice. Friendly, and thanked me for the cake. It went well.'

'So why are you blushing?'

'I'm not, I'm just feeling a bit harassed this morning. Lots to do, and I keep getting distracted. First at Minnie's shop, then in Eila's shop. I haven't even sorted my meringues yet.'

Judy eyed him, knowing him well enough to surmise that something had happened. 'Is she pretty?'

Gordon went behind the counter and started to rearrange the cupcakes on display. 'She is, very pretty.'

Judy smiled at him.

'I gave her the cake, she thanked me, and that was it,' he summarised.

'You're editing the good bits.' Judy encouraged him to tell her what happened.

'She's seen me swimming in the mornings. I didn't know. She said she didn't recognise me at first with my clothes on.'

Judy laughed. 'Well, it sounds like you may have an admirer.'

Gordon brushed this suggestion aside. 'No, I don't think so, but it made things momentarily embarrassing for both of us.'

'You were wearing swimming trunks, so at least she hasn't seen your wee whistle.'

'Judy!'

She laughed again. 'There's going to be plenty of gossip at the bee tonight, so be prepared to be one of the hot topics.'

'I'm sure you'll have enough to chatter about because of Sholto.'

As if she suddenly realised the time, Judy jolted. 'I'd better be off to help Pearl.' She smiled at him and hurried out.

Gordon sighed heavily. It was going to be one of those days.

Judy dashed into the dress shop. 'Hello, Eila. All the best with your new shop. I'm Judy. My husband, Jock, and I own the bar restaurant next to Gordon's tea shop. The quilting bee ladies were intending to pop along today to support you, but we've got to help Pearl get the big house ready.'

Judy seemed keyed up, so whatever had her in a tizzy had to be important.

'Four rich, successful and gorgeous men are coming here this weekend,' Judy announced.

'Rich, successful and gorgeous men? Is that bad?'

'Yes, they're scoundrels! Not in business, but in romance and their dealings with women. They're hard to resist. So don't say you haven't been warned. We'll explain everything tonight. See you at seven.'

Part of Eila was glad she'd kept herself tucked away while setting up her business. In the current whirlwind she'd have managed to get very little done.

As Judy went to hurry out, she halted when she noticed the new embroidery threads on display.

'Are those the new season's colours?' Judy asked.

'Yes, Pearl said she liked them.'

'I'll definitely be buying some of those, but I like to dwell on the colours, so I'll be back when I'm not in a hurry,' said Judy. 'Don't worry if you see a few of us scurrying back and forth. We're all pitching in to help Pearl clean the house.'

With a quick wave, Judy ran away.

Eila smiled to herself, wondering if her evening at the quilting bee would be as hectic.

CHAPTER THREE

Pearl and Judy took an end each of the large white cloth that covered the table in the dining room of Sholto's house.

'You fold your end towards me,' Pearl instructed. 'Keep it tight so that any stoor isn't thrown all over the floor. There's enough hoovering to be done.'

Judy helped Pearl fold the cloth, and then they tackled several other dust covers on the chairs and dressers.

Judy admired the decor while they worked. 'It is a beautiful house. Far too big for my taste, but I can appreciate the grandeur.'

'Josh's mansion is substantial, but not as big as this house. Trees and shrubs provide privacy for Josh, but there's a spectacular view of the sea from the second–floor balcony. Sholto's property is hidden by trees and greenery.'

'I prefer Josh's house,' said Judy, referring to one of the local residents. Josh was a rich businessman and owned the two–storey house. He'd recently become romantically involved with Abby who'd come to live and work in one of the cottages down by the shore.

'So do I,' Pearl agreed. She worked as a part–time housekeeper for Josh.

'When are Abby and Josh coming home?'

'Abby phoned Minnie the other day. She's having a lovely time in New York with Josh. Obviously, he's there on businesses, but they're making a holiday out of the trip.'

'New York, eh? I've never been there. Jock wanted us to go there on honeymoon years ago, but then we decided we had everything we needed right here in Scotland. We had a trip through the Highlands. It was a great time.'

Pearl's phone rang. 'It's Minnie,' she said to Judy.

'I'm closing my shop for a couple of hours,' said Minnie. 'I'll be there to help you soon. Is there anything you need me to bring with me?'

'No, I've got tons of cleaning stuff. Just bring the elbow grease,' Pearl replied.

'I'm on my way,' chirped Minnie.

Three other ladies from the quilting bee had arrived and were getting torn into hoovering the bedrooms and putting fresh linen on the beds.

Pearl sighed. 'It's not right that Sholto's put me in this position.'

'It's the position Sholto and his sons will put the local women in that's my concern,' said Judy.

Pearl dusted down the dresser and straightened one of the expensive paintings on the dining room wall. 'I'm grateful for all the help. But my feathers are fizzing.'

'Don't upset yourself. We all understand,' Judy assured her.

'Sholto's causing merry chaos and he hasn't even arrived yet!'

Judy climbed up a step ladder and flicked a duster over the droplets hanging from the crystal chandelier. 'Maybe they're not half as handsome as they used to be. We could be remembering them in a rosy glow.'

'I hadn't considered that,' Pearl mused, checking that the silver was still in the dresser drawer. Catering staff had been hired and they'd do the polishing of the silver, and it all seemed to be present and accounted for.

'Mind you,' Judy added, 'Cairn's got a manly beauty. He's the type to wear well. With his blond hair, any glitter strands will blend in. Not that I'd be able to have a close–up look at Cairn's hair. He's so tall.'

'They're all tall. It emphasises them looking down on us. In more ways than one.' Pearl pulled the ceiling to floor length burgundy brocade curtains aside from the edges of the windows and secured them with tassel tiebacks.

'I refuse to let them look down their snooty noses at me.' The chandelier tinkled as Judy flicked the dust away. They'd been recently cleaned and only needed a quick flick.

Pearl looked around. 'The house has been well maintained. There's a lot of work to be done, but it's been regularly dusted and hoovered, so it's more setting everything up without the dust covers. Making it look like home.'

Judy eyed the expensive furnishings that screamed class from every niche. 'But it'll never feel homely.'

'Where are you?' Minnie's voice echoed through the vast house.

'We're in here,' Pearl called to her.

Minnie walked in, armed with an apron with deep pockets and a scarf to tie around her hair. 'I'd forgotten how grand this house is.' She gazed at the vast main lounge that doubled as a small ballroom.

'It's been a long time since we were all here at that last dance Sholto had before he packed up and left.' There was a bitter tone in Pearl's voice. 'No notice given. Luckily, there was work available for me locally, including at Josh's house.'

'No consideration,' Minnie snipped, helping to polish the antique dresser that she'd always admired. 'Leave without notice, and arrive in the same way. Sheer arrogance.'

'Any more gossip about Sholto's sons?' Judy asked.

'Neither of them have married, or come close to settling down,' Pearl told her. 'Hamish was dating a woman in Edinburgh, a businesswoman, but that fizzled out when he realised she was just after his money to help her expand her firm.'

'What about Fraser?' said Minnie. 'Didn't their mother have high hopes that the younger son would join her catering business?'

'Sholto's wife is barely mentioned these days,' Pearl confided. 'Not since the scandalous incident with the French chef.'

'The icing and the spatula thing?' said Judy.

Pearl nodded. 'After the swift divorce, Sholto banned all discussion involving their mother. Fraser had trained up to a certain level as a chef, and she'd planned to train him further as a chocolatier or patisserie chef. But those plans were halted by Sholto. He got the sons, and his wife got the short end of the stick.'

'His wife is powerful in her own right,' Judy remarked.

'She does well for herself,' Pearl agreed. 'I've heard she didn't weep any tears over her split from Sholto, but they still clash from time to time when they have family business to discuss. It's all done by phone or email. They never meet up.'

Minnie polished a dresser that had an ornate lamp on it. 'None of them seem very happy.'

The others agreed.

'Cairn has never married either,' Pearl continued. 'I don't think he's the marrying kind.'

'He's an icy one.' Minnie shivered. 'Even if I was younger, I couldn't imagine dating a man like Cairn. He's a looker, but I couldn't picture having a cosy night in with him.'

'Cosy and Cairn are two words rarely uttered,' said Pearl.

'Has Sholto ever considered remarrying?' asked Judy.

'Nooo.' Pearl sounded sure of this. 'I doubt he'll walk down the aisle again with any woman.'

Minnie used some of that elbow grease to polish the dresser. 'I wish they hadn't decided to come back here. I was looking forward to a long, relaxing, end of summer time. Only a few more weeks and it'll be autumn.'

'We'll still enjoy it,' said Judy. 'Once the house is clean and ready, and the troublemakers are entrenched here, we can ignore the lot of them, as they like to ignore us.'

'You're right,' Minnie agreed. 'It's not as if they'll be inviting us to one of their posh balls.'

'We were all at the last one,' Pearl reminded her. 'That was quite a night.'

'We were,' Minnie acknowledged, 'but I think Sholto invited the locals because we were always accusing him of cold shouldering us. I think he did it to spite us, and an invitation given in that manner is never right.'

'I remember that night.' Euan's voice sounded in the hallway as he walked in. His shirt sleeves were rolled up and he was holding a garden trowel. 'I think I danced with all of you.'

Minnie smiled. 'You did. Unlike Sholto, Hamish and Fraser.'

'My Jock danced with quite a few women,' Judy added.

'Jock's a fine dancer,' said Minnie. 'Is he still intending to keep his ceilidh dance nights going at the bar restaurant?'

'He is,' Judy confirmed. 'They're very popular. He's happy to give lessons too.'

'Jock showed me how to improve my dancing for the ceilidh,' said Euan, smiling at the thought of it. 'And he taught your boyfriend, Shawn, how to waggle his kilt,' he added, looking at Minnie.

'Shawn's not my boyfriend.' Minnie looked ruffled. 'We're friends.'

Pearl and Judy exchanged a knowing look, and Euan smiled.

'Okay, so maybe we're extra friendly sometimes,' Minnie relented. 'But I'm not thinking of getting into any serious romantic relationships. I like my life the way it is.'

Several other women turned up and soon the house was looking spick and span.

Euan tidied the garden, and later on everyone sat together in the sunshine to have a cup of tea and biscuits.

'Eila's coming along to the quilting bee tonight,' Judy told Minnie. 'She has a wonderful selection of new embroidery thread.'

'Did you see the colours?' Pearl added. 'I'm going to buy a few of them for my embroidery. It'll be so handy having the thread in her shop instead of needing to travel into the town to buy it.'

'We'll need to warn her about Sholto and his sons,' said Minnie. 'I'd hate to see her hurt by any of them.'

'Gordon seemed quite taken with her,' Judy commented.

'Did he now?' Minnie smirked.

'He gave her a cake for her opening day,' Judy explained. 'I kept an eye on the tea shop while he popped along. He was only gone for a few minutes, but when he came back his face was rosy flushed. I think he fancies her.'

'It would be lovely if Gordon found himself a nice young woman,' said Minnie.

Judy continued to explain what Eila had said about seeing Gordon in his swimming trunks.

The women laughed.

'Gordon's a fine looking young man,' said Pearl.

'We'll see if there are any sparks flying between Gordon and Eila tonight,' Minnie said, smiling.

'But we won't interfere with any potential romance,' Judy added firmly. 'You know the trouble we can cause, intentional or not, when we meddle.'

Minnie nodded.

And then they all laughed again.

After their tea break, the other women headed home, leaving Pearl, Minnie and Judy to check the last bits and pieces.

Euan had tidied the garden sufficiently, and drove off to get on with his own work.

Pearl stood in the main hallway. 'Well, I think it's ready for them arriving.'

'Are the caterers stocking the kitchen with groceries?' Minnie asked.

'I believe so,' Pearl confirmed. 'Sholto has hired some local staff to deal with that side of things.'

'Will you need any help tomorrow?' Judy asked Pearl.

'No, but thanks.' Pearl sighed with relief. 'With everyone pitching in, there are only a few wee futtery jobs that need done, and I'll do them in the morning. We've done enough for one day.'

The glow of a languid sunny evening shone into the house.

'We should head back and get cleaned up in time for our bee night.' Minnie took her apron off. 'Gordon's promised to bake extra chocolate cakes for us.'

'Gordon's a warm–hearted, kind sort of man,' said Pearl. 'Not like that cold–hearted Cairn.'

Judy shrugged the tiredness from her shoulders. 'Cairn has beautiful eyes for a man, but they can cut right through you.'

'I'd be surprised if Cairn even has a heart,' Minnie said snippily. Her voice resounded in the vast hallway.

'Good–evening, ladies,' Cairn's voice clashed with Minnie's comment and caused the women to look round and gasp when they saw him standing there.

Cairn wore an immaculate suit, and although his blond hair and tall, lean, broad–shouldered stature was bathed in the glow of the early evening sun, everything about him sent a cold chill through the women.

Pearl was startled and fumbled, dropping her bag.

Cairn stepped forward, picked it up and handed it to her, icing her to the core with a look.

Pearl was too taken aback to thank him. 'I thought you weren't arriving until Saturday.'

'Sholto asked me to come here early and check that everything was in order,' Cairn told her.

'There's no food in the house,' Pearl said, sounding ruffled.

'I'll manage, Pearl,' Cairn told her.

'My restaurant is open this evening,' said Judy.

'I won't be dining there tonight, Judy.' Cairn's tone gave no hint of what his plans were.

A tense silence turned the air to ice, before Minnie spoke up. 'You can pick up groceries from my shop until I close in just over an hour's time.'

Cairn's firm lips almost formed into a smile. 'I'll keep that in mind, Minnie.'

The women gave each other a look and then made their way out together.

'Everything else should be in order for you to be comfortable sleeping here tonight,' Pearl told him before she left. 'I'll pop back in the morning to sort a few things.'

'You've managed to do a lot of work in a short amount of time, Pearl,' he remarked.

'Minnie and Judy helped me, along with other women from the quilting bee,' Pearl explained. 'It was short notice to get a house this size ready.'

'And Euan worked all day tidying your garden,' Minnie chipped in.

Cairn seemed to absorb all this information, but his cold demeanour gave nothing away.

'Is there a problem with my friends helping me?' Pearl asked Cairn.

'Yes, everyone will be paid for their work,' Cairn told her.

'We're not looking for payment,' Judy stated.

Minnie nodded.

'I understand that,' Cairn said, 'but it's only fair that they be paid. I'll have money paid into your account, Pearl. I'll leave it up to you to divide it out accordingly.'

A stunned silence filled the hallway as the women stood at the entrance, ready to leave.

'Thank you, Cairn,' Pearl finally managed to say. 'I'll see you in the morning.'

Nodding firmly, Cairn then watched them walk away.

'We'll talk about this tonight,' Minnie whispered to Pearl and Judy. 'I think Cairn is watching us, so act calm and cheerful. Don't let him see we're perturbed.'

'He remembered all of our names,' Judy hissed.

Minnie nodded, wondering what else Cairn remembered about them. Smiling and waving to each other, the women drove off in their cars, heading away from the house back down to the seashore.

Minnie opened up her shop and several customers came in to buy groceries for their dinner.

After serving them, Minnie closed the shop for the night and got ready for the quilting bee.

As promised, Gordon had baked extra chocolate cakes for the bee members, and as the women filtered in, carrying their sewing bags and other craft items, he brought their tea, cakes and scones through. He'd added a selection of his latest chocolates to the cake stands.

The function room had folding tables that he set up for the quilting bee evenings. The tables and chairs were positioned to allow the members to enjoy sewing and have their evening tea. Gordon let them keep their machines in the back of the function room to save lugging them there twice a week for the bee nights.

On warm evenings he opened the patio doors that led out to the garden, allowing fresh air to waft in. On colder evenings the vintage lamps with their pink and amber glass shades created a bright but cosy atmosphere.

Minnie and Judy were sitting together relaying the events of the day to other members when Pearl came hurrying in.

'Sholto's been very generous in paying for the work we all did,' Pearl announced. She sat down beside Minnie and Judy.

'I'm not looking for any payment,' Judy told her.

Pearl brushed this aside. 'I'm going to divide it up fairly. I've messaged Euan and told him he'll get his share.'

As they were talking, Euan walked in, making his way through the tea shop to the function room.

'I got your message, Pearl, but I don't need any money from Cairn.'

Euan was quite wealthy in his own right, not in the same league as Sholto, but rich enough.

Pearl explained that she planned to divide out the money.

Euan stopped her when she repeated that he would be included. 'No, Pearl. I'm fine. Share my payment out with the others, or add it to your quilting bee fund.'

'That's a great idea,' said Pearl. 'Are you sure?'

Euan nodded firmly.

'Thank you, Euan. I'll add it to our fund.' Pearl smiled and the others appreciated his generosity.

'I'll not hang around,' Euan said, and bid them goodnight.

The members continued chatting about everything that had happened, when Eila joined them. She was carrying a bag with her sewing in it, and another bag filled with fabric.

Minnie welcomed her in and introduced her to the members.

Eila was seated beside Minnie and the others and given a cup of tea.

Quilts were being hand stitched and machined by members of the bee, and she noticed that members were also sewing other items, embroidering and knitting. But there was a sense that something had happened and the ladies were buzzing with the news.

'Is everything okay?' asked Eila.

Minnie sighed. 'I'll give you the short course on what's happened...'

'Cairn arrived early?' Eila said, after hearing Minnie's version of events.

'We were caught off guard,' Minnie explained. 'We're going to enjoy our bee night, but we'll also have to come up with a plan of action.'

Eila frowned. 'Cairn sounds quite formidable.'

Pearl joined in. 'He is.'

'Thankfully, they don't like to fraternise with the locals, and tend to keep themselves to themselves up at Sholto's house,' said Minnie.

'Probably best if we all get on with our own business,' Eila commented.

'Yes,' Minnie agreed. 'But we'll need contingency plans in case things go awry. There's a tendency for that to happen around here.'

One of the members sewing hexies to make a quilt asked, 'Was Cairn has handsome as he used to be?'

'Oh, yes,' Minnie told her, as the other women listened to every detail. 'And as immaculate as ever in his expensive suit.'

'He's a beautiful man,' Judy said reluctantly. 'That blond hair and those ice blue eyes of his are lethal. I know what he's like, and I still found myself holding my breath just looking at him.'

'He's not my type,' Eila told them. 'I prefer warm–hearted men with darker hair and a friendly attitude.'

'So do I,' Judy agreed. 'Men like my Jock. But I defy you to stand near Cairn and not feel your heart flutter, even though you'd prefer it not to.'

CHAPTER FOUR

Gordon hurried through from the front of the tea shop where he was busy serving customers their suppers. On bee nights he kept the premises open late.

He went over to Eila and smiled. 'Have you had your dinner? Or can I offer you some supper?'

Eila smiled up at him. 'I got caught up in things at my shop. I haven't gotten into the swing of things, and before I knew it, the time had flown and I rushed over here to the quilting bee.'

'So you'll be a wee bit hungry then?' said Gordon.

Eila nodded, wondering what type of suppers were available. She'd never been a fussy eater and was willing to have whatever was going.

'I've made my special cheese and tomato quiche,' he said.

'That sounds great.'

'Salad to go with it?' he added.

'Yes, thank you, Gordon.' Eila smiled as Gordon hurried away to get her supper.

'I think you've made quite the impression on our Gordon,' Judy commented.

Eila felt a blush rise in her cheeks and tried to keep calm, but the busy bee night was bustling with activity, chatter, tea and tasty treats, and she was in the middle of the cosy hub.

'I heard that you didn't recognise Gordon with his clothes on,' one of the other members remarked.

Eila blushed rosy pink. 'I haven't been deliberately watching him, but it's hard not to notice him swimming in the sea when I'm admiring the view out of my shop window.'

'Gordon creates a lovely view, doesn't he, ladies?' Pearl said, smiling and teasing Eila.

Realising that everything was said in a light–hearted manner made Eila feel part of their fun–filled evening.

Gordon served Eila her supper, and she enjoyed it amid the gossip and whirring of sewing machines.

‘This quiche is delicious,’ Eila said, tucking into it. She hadn’t realised how hungry she was. Gordon had been lavish with the sprinkled cheese and spring onion topping.

‘Gordon always lays on a lovely selection of cakes, scones, flans and chocolate treats for our evening tea,’ Minnie told her. ‘He trained as a chef in Glasgow.’

‘So he’s from the city?’ said Eila.

‘Yes, he’s a bit like you. He’s only been here a wee while, but he’s settled in well.’

‘The vintage decor is lovely,’ Eila remarked, admiring the tea shop.

Minnie nodded. ‘Gordon bought the tea shop when the previous owners retired and he kept a lot of the original decor. He modernised the kitchen, but the vintage decor adds to the atmosphere.’

‘I noticed that there are stairs leading up to a second floor,’ said Eila. ‘Is that another part of the tea shop? A restaurant?’

‘No, Gordon lives upstairs,’ Minnie explained. ‘It’s beautiful. Ideal for a single man.’

‘Yes, he’s single,’ Judy emphasised, leaning close and whispering. ‘We’re not wishing to meddle, but are you dating anyone?’

‘No, I’ve never been lucky in that respect. I haven’t dated anyone for a couple of years. I’ve been busy building up my business.’

‘Have you always been into dressmaking?’ Pearl asked her.

‘Yes, I love to sew and design dresses and skirts. I’ve brought a wrap around skirt with me tonight to stitch.’ Eila opened her sewing bag and lifted the skirt out to show them what she was working on. ‘It’s one of my most popular patterns. The wrap around skirts fit all sizes and are comfy to wear.’ Eila was wearing one, a lovely light floral print, teamed with a pretty blouse.

The women admired her work, and many had viewed her designs on her website.

‘I enjoy making dresses,’ said Judy. ‘But the quality of your designs is exceptional. It’s like they’re precision cut by a top tailor and stitched to perfection.’

‘My father is a tailor,’ Eila told them. ‘My mother loved to sew, but she passed when I was very little and I don’t really remember her. I was brought up by my father and learned to sew from him.’

'Ah, so that's where you get your skill,' Minnie remarked.

Eila nodded. 'He was born on one of the islands where his father and grandfather were involved in the making of classic fabrics for men's suits. Then he moved to the city to expand his career. That's where he met my mother. He's in London now, still working as a tailor. He wanted me to move to London with him, but I've never felt that I could settle there. Although I was brought up in Glasgow, I always dreamed of moving away to set up home beside the sea.'

Gordon wasn't deliberately eavesdropping on the women's conversation, but he couldn't help overhearing Eila telling them about her background. He wasn't an expert in sewing, but he had admired the dresses in Eila's window display. She certainly had a talent for designing and making beautiful dresses.

He found himself hoping that her shop would thrive and that she would stay. He liked, Eila, but despite the almost instant attraction he felt for her, he didn't plan on asking her out on a date so soon. He'd let her settle into things, get to know her and give her time to get to know him.

'I brought the fabric bundles for you.' Eila dug them out of her bag and handed them to Pearl.

'Oh, thank you.' Pearl showed the other women what she'd bought and promised to settle up with Eila in the morning.

'I'm so glad you sell fat quarter bundles of quilting weight cotton,' Minnie enthused. 'You'll do a roaring trade from us. We buy online, but we also like to pop to the nearest town and buy fabric there. But if you're selling selections like this, we'll buy it from you. Where do you source your material? It's lovely.'

'I scour around for my fabric and have several reliable suppliers that make wonderful selections. I try to buy from their latest collections as well as the classics. It keeps things fresh and exciting.'

The fat quarter bundles were passed around the members and then handed back to Pearl. A few of them asked Eila to put bundles aside for them.

Eila then brought out a card with samples of embroidery thread and gave it to Judy. 'I thought you'd like to have a look at the new colours.'

Judy accepted it with glee. 'I love colour cards like these.'

The embroidery thread sample card was then passed around the members to their delight.

'I'm not looking to ply my trade,' Eila emphasised. 'I want to be part of the quilting bee. I just thought I'd do this tonight.'

'We're happy for you to do this, Eila,' Minnie assured her. 'We all show our work at the bee.'

Gordon approached with a plate of chocolate treats. 'I know you're careful of having sticky or chocolate fingers when you're handling your sewing. But these are my new chocolate bonbons. They're filled with ganache. Would you like to try one?' He offered them around.

Eila bit into one of them and sighed. 'This is so delicious.'

The other ladies agreed, but it was Eila that he was particularly eager to impress.

'I've seen your chocolate selection in the tea shop window,' said Eila. 'Do you make them all yourself?'

Gordon smiled. 'I do. I've found a new way to handle my bonbons. I'd be happy to give you a demonstration.'

Eila tried not to laugh, and smiled and nodded.

Gordon left them to enjoy the chocolates.

Judy nudged Eila. 'There's an offer, eh?'

The women giggled, and so did Eila, enjoying the fun of the evening.

They were still laughing, discussing the new fabrics and embroidery thread, and eating the bonbons when the happy atmosphere suddenly changed.

'Don't look now, but there's Cairn,' Minnie whispered to the women.

Eila looked round towards the front of the tea shop, and there was a tall, blond and incredibly handsome man standing there. Even from where she was sitting she could see that the suit he wore was tailored to perfection. He wore it well, very well, and her heart skipped a beat as he glanced at her.

Wow, Cairn was handsome, Eila thought, and now he was walking through to the hub of the quilting bee, and seemed to be targeting her!

Gordon noticed Cairn making a beeline for Eila, and stepped in, cutting him off at the pass. He couldn't be sure that this was Cairn, but he'd heard the women saying Cairn had arrived early, and he fitted their description.

'Are you in for supper?' Gordon asked Cairn, standing in front of him, preventing him heading through to the bee. 'Suppers are available in the front of the tea shop. The function room is booked for the quilting bee members.'

'I'm looking for Pearl,' said Cairn.

Gordon blinked, thinking he'd misread Cairn's objective.

Cairn iced Gordon with a look. 'I need to talk to Pearl.' This was partially true, but Eila was his main target. He recognised her from the pictures on her website that he'd just seen. He wanted to assess her for a few moments before making his approach.

Gordon reluctantly stepped aside, allowing Cairn to brush past him and walk into the hub of the bee.

Silence fell over the happy evening as the chatter faded and the sewing machines stopped whirring.

Cairn looked at Eila then forced himself to focus on Pearl. 'I wanted to check that you received the payment.'

'I did, thank you, and I'm dividing it between the women as agreed. Euan didn't want payment, but I insisted, so he's donated it to our quilting bee fund.'

'As long as everyone is satisfied with this, that's fine,' Cairn told Pearl.

The women waited, thinking that Cairn would now leave, but he lingered, causing a feeling of tension. His eyes flicked a glance a few times towards Eila, and finally Minnie made the introduction.

'Cairn, this is Eila. She's opened a new dress shop here.'

Eila acknowledged Cairn with a polite nod.

'I've just seen your dress shop. It's the one further along the esplanade. I'd like to talk to you if you have a few minutes to spare.' Cairn's words hung in the air as Eila hesitated.

'Eila is enjoying our quilting bee night,' Minnie told him firmly.

'I'm aware that I'm interrupting, but this won't take long,' Cairn replied.

Sensing the atmosphere becoming more awkward, Eila stood up. 'Okay.'

'You don't have to go,' Minnie told her, and then glared at Cairn.

The glaring daggers bounced off Cairn's cold exterior. He was used to others trying to thwart him. It never worked.

Cairn led the way out of the function room through to the front of the tea shop.

Eila followed him, glancing back and giving Minnie a reassuring nod.

As they walked past Gordon he voiced his objections. 'You can't come in here and disrupt the women's evening. And I was about to serve them more chocolates.'

Gordon's objection made no impact on Cairn's intention to leave with Eila.

Eila eyed Gordon, hoping that her expression assured him she was fine.

'Well! Would you look at that!' Minnie gasped, hurrying through and peering out the tea shop window.

'What did Cairn say to Eila?' Gordon asked Minnie, as several of the women joined her and peered outside.

'He said he saw her dress shop and wants to talk to her for a few minutes,' Minnie replied.

Gordon looked angry and annoyed, pacing outside, watching them walk away to the dress shop.

Minnie looked at Judy and Pearl. 'What do you think we should do?'

'I'm reluctant to interfere,' said Pearl.

Judy nodded. 'We agreed that we wouldn't meddle in Eila's personal business.'

Minnie huffed. 'Yes, but we didn't expect Cairn to waltz into the bee and whisk her away with him.'

'What is he up to?' Gordon sounded distressed. 'Eila doesn't know what a man like Cairn is capable of. He wields his handsome looks like a weapon.'

Minnie brought out her phone. 'I'll text her. Her number was on her website. I've got it locked and loaded.'

Eila walked along with Cairn towards her shop. She barely came up to his shoulders and the confidence in his manner was as breathtaking as he was. Judy was right. The fluttering of her heart was increasing the longer she was near him. Calm down, she scolded herself.

Getting a grip, she challenged him. 'Would you like to tell me what you're up to?'

Her bluntness startled him, though she would never know. He didn't flinch, and continued to walk steadily towards the shop.

'I didn't know there was a dress shop here,' he began. 'I'd checked the businesses listed, but yours wasn't included.' His tone seemed to require an explanation from her, so she obliged.

'This is my first day opening. I've only been here a couple of weeks, so your business information probably hasn't been updated.'

Cairn nodded. 'I saw your name and website on the window. I checked your website before going along to the tea shop. I hoped I'd find you there. The quilting bee nights tend to attract every woman like moths to a flame. I knocked, but your shop was in darkness. You were clearly out. It was a fair bet where you'd be.'

'You still haven't answered my question.' She had no intention of backing down. He reminded her of haughty, wealthy men she'd met in the past, and wasn't fazed by his attitude.

'The items in the front window interested me.'

She frowned. 'What items?' Her mind rewound the rush she'd been in earlier, realising the window was almost empty after selling most of the dresses. Customers had come in to browse and buy during the day. She'd done quite well. But it was the online sales that had taken a leap and practically emptied her main stock. She'd parcelled up the dress and skirt orders and ran to the post office with them. Another thing she'd have to get used to — the times when orders were picked up at the post office.

'The jackets and waistcoats.' His tone sounded crisp in the night air.

'I put them in the window rather than leave it empty,' she explained. 'I'd sold several dresses, my popular designs, and as I said, this was my first day opening. I've yet to settle in and find a method for restocking quickly. I only hung the jackets and waistcoats up temporarily.'

'Do you sell many of the jackets?'

'No, I concentrate mainly on the dresses. The jackets require a lot more work and are not as cost effective as other items.' She paused. 'But I do love making them.'

'They're excellent. First class.'

His compliments were still lingering in the air as they arrived outside the shop.

Eila dug her keys out of her bag and unlocked the door.

Cairn gazed in the window. 'The cut of that jacket is classic. The fabric is perfect.' His eyes then looked right at her. 'The cut and fabric are everything.'

And then he followed her inside the shop.

She closed the door as the sea breeze was whipping along the esplanade, picking up pace, as was her heart rate. Seeing the beautifully handsome and imposing stature of Cairn standing in her shop diminished its size. Or perhaps she was feeling the effects of this man as Judy and the other women had warned her.

Despite trying to remain unaffected by him, she couldn't prevent herself from feeling impressed by him. So far, he'd done nothing to upset her.

She stood there and faced him, gazing up, trying to appear confident. She was confident, she told herself, but Cairn was disconcerting.

'May I take a closer look at the jackets and waistcoats?'

'Yes.'

She watched him go over, seeming eager, and lift them from the window display and place them on the counter. He proceeded to inspect everything from the lining to the top stitching on the pockets. The silk back waistcoats were scrutinised by him under the lights.

'Excellent work, Eila.'

Hearing him say her name sent shivers through her. Not in a cold way. Cairn affected her, but then, he'd affect most women.

'Did you do all the cutting yourself?' he asked, holding up one of the jackets and checking the lapels and pockets.

'I do. I'm fussy about cutting the fabric.'

'Where did you train?'

'My father is a tailor. I learned from him.'

Cairn became thoughtful. 'Your name on the window and in the website seemed vaguely familiar. I've probably encountered your father's work. The tailoring business is a big small world.'

'My father used to say that. He had a reputation for being one of the top cutters at one time.'

'Is he retired now?'

'No, he's based in London, and specialises in making bespoke suits for specific clients.'

Cairn nodded. 'Yes, I've probably seen his work. But it's your work, your selection of fabric that's of interest to me.' He put the jacket down and moved closer until he was standing right in front of her, gazing down. 'Would you be prepared to share with me where you source your fabrics?'

'I source my fabrics from a handful of suppliers. I'd be happy to give you a list.'

'You'll be paid accordingly.'

'I don't need paid, Cairn. I'll give you the list. Any fabric you purchase from them will help keep their businesses thriving. And that will ensure I can continue buying from them. Everyone benefits.'

Cairn frowned, and she noticed how beautiful his face really was. Even when vexed, he was the most handsome person she'd ever seen.

'Are you okay?' he asked.

She blinked out of her thoughts. 'Yes.'

'You'd stopped breathing there. I wondered what was wrong?'

'Nothing. It's been a whirlwind day, and I'd been hoping to relax at the quilting bee.'

'Ah, yes, I'm keeping you from your evening.'

'I can email the list to you later.'

He nodded and they exchanged contact details. She saw the message from Minnie.

Everything okay? Be careful around Cairn.

I'm fine, thanks, she replied.

Eila put the phone away and watched Cairn. He was looking at the rolls of fabric on the shelves. Not the flowery prints. The worsted wool, tweed, linen and gabardine. Some were plain, relying on the texture, while others had a pin stripe or fine check pattern. The herringbone in muted blue caught his interest, and he pulled the roll out to study the quality of the fabric.

'I'd really like to discuss your fabric choices, the colours — are they new?'

'The colours are part of new collections. I like to work with the classic neutrals and warm amber and autumn tones, and muted greens. But these new blue and pink tones are lovely.'

For a moment Cairn looked at Eila. 'Very lovely.'

She blushed and tried to walk past him to show him other designs she was working on.

'I don't mean to cause you any trouble,' he said earnestly.

‘You’re not,’ she lied.

CHAPTER FIVE

Gordon looked concerned. 'What do you think Cairn is up to with Eila?'

Minnie and the other ladies were busy sewing and chatting, but no one could really settle.

'Eila says everything's fine,' Minnie told him. 'But I wonder if I should pop along to check on her.'

'What does he want from her dress shop at this time of night?' Pearl sounded irate. 'Cairn's a slippery customer. He's bound to be up to no good.'

Judy looked worried. 'Eila's a confident young woman, but Cairn can't be trusted. I'm not suggesting he's going to jump on her. None of them were ever like that, forcing themselves on the local ladies. But they knew how to use their looks to full advantage.'

Minnie put her sewing down and stood up. 'Right, I'm going along to see if Eila's okay. She's been gone for half an hour. She didn't even get a sniff of her chocolate cake or fruit scone.'

'I'll go with you,' Gordon offered.

'No, it's better if I go myself. You might get into a fight with him, and we don't want any fisticuffs.'

'What fight? What fisticuffs?' Judy's husband, Jock, demanded to know as he walked in on their conversation.

Judy raised her hand to calm her husband. 'There's no trouble. We're just concerned about Eila being alone in her dress shop with Cairn.'

Jock was taken aback. 'She's in the shop with him just now?' Jock started to march out of the function room. 'I'll settle Cairn's hash for him!'

'No, Jock.' Judy hurried after him. She'd told him about Cairn's arrival at the house, sparking his jealousy. Her husband was generally an easy–going man, but he knew the effect Cairn had on Judy, even though he trusted her implicitly.

Jock wouldn't be stopped and stomped out of the tea shop. 'Sholto and his heartbreaking clique can't waltz into our lives again and cause ructions.'

Gordon hurried after Jock.

With Jock leading the way, several others, including Gordon, marched along to the dress shop.

Eila was showing Cairn her notebooks filled with designs. She kept them in her living room. Her laptop was set up on a table near the fireplace, and several notebooks were tucked up on a shelf.

She'd cut pieces of the fabrics she'd used for dressmaking, and stuck them into large notebooks. Details of the fabrics — colours, texture and usage were written beside each piece.

Cairn poured through one of the notebooks, admiring her designs, and was especially interested in her colour combinations. 'These are a refreshing take on the classics. You have a great eye for colour and combining textures.'

She smiled at him, warming to the obvious coldness in him. 'I enjoy making them. They're like journals or scrapbooks. I love sticking pieces of fabric in them and making notes. I started doing this when learning tailoring from my father. The suit fabrics have a wonderful quality and texture. So different from the lighter cottons I use for dressmaking.'

'These are of interest to me. I'd like to talk to you more about them. Could we discuss things in more detail tomorrow?'

'I'll be busy in my shop during the day,' she reminded him.

He nodded. 'I understand. But could you have dinner with me tomorrow night up at the house? We could discuss things further over dinner.'

She found herself nodding without thinking things through properly. Dinner with Cairn?

'I'll pay you for your time and any information of yours that I use.'

She went to object, but he insisted.

'Can I ask,' she said, 'what's the real reason Sholto is coming back here?'

'The business is not in trouble, if that's what you're thinking.'

She had considered this.

'Sholto has always kept ahead of the game, shall we say, when it comes to business. The last few collections have done well, but he feels as if we're stuck in a rut and need to shake ourselves to do better. He thinks we're heavily influenced by the city, and that a change of scene, back to his original home where his business began, would be of benefit.'

'So here you are.'

Cairn nodded. 'His sons, Hamish and Fraser didn't want to pack up and move here, even if it's only for a few weeks.'

'Did you?' she asked him.

'No, I didn't. But having arrived ahead of them, and felt the change of scene immediately, perhaps Sholto is right.' He tapped his hand on one of her design notebooks. 'It's my job to scout for new ideas, a fresh approach, as well as theirs. When I saw your shop, the tailored jackets and waistcoats, the new fabric and colours...I thought it would be great to have something of interest to Sholto to show him by the time he arrives.'

'How long have you worked for Sholto?'

'Since I started my career in tailoring years ago.'

'You're a tailor yourself, not just Sholto's assistant?'

'Yes, but it's a difficult business to strike out on, if you're on your own, without enormous talent. I didn't think I was talented enough, but as part of Sholto's company, I found my perfect niche.'

'Is your family's background in tailoring?' She wondered if his past was similar to hers.

'No, they're in banking, finance, and disappointed that I didn't join the family business.' He saw the look in her eyes and recognised it instantly. He'd seen people's reaction to this before. 'So yes, I come from money. I have my own inherited wealth apart from my success with Sholto.'

'*Four rich, successful and gorgeous men...*' Eila remembered Judy's description of them. Now here she was with one of them, and now had a dinner date with Cairn.

Jock hammered his fist on the dress shop door. The shop was lit up, but there was no sign of Eila or Cairn. 'Eila, open up. Are you okay in there, lass?'

Minnie and Judy exchanged a worried glance.

'Where is she?' said Minnie, clutching her cardigan.

Gordon hurried round the back of the property. The back garden was in shadowed darkness, lit only by the light shining out the back windows from the cottage.

He cupped his hand and peered in the living room window and saw Cairn standing there looking at swatches of fabric while Eila chatted animatedly.

Gordon's blood boiled, thinking Cairn was pretending to be interested in Eila's dressmaking. Using his wiles to encourage her to drop her guard.

Then two things happened...

Eila must've heard Jock at the front door, and left Cairn holding the fabric samples while she went to answer it...

But as she looked round, she saw a strange man peering in the window at her. She shrieked, getting a fright, seeing him staring at her. It took a moment before she realised it was Gordon, and even then she didn't immediately calm down, especially as Jock was shouting through to her and hammering on the front door.

Glaring at Gordon, she then ran through to the shop and opened the door.

Jock and the others poured it.

'Where is he?' Jock demanded. 'Where's the rascal?'

Surmising he was the cause of the whole kerfuffle, Cairn stared at Gordon and then walked through to confront the trouble.

'What are you up to with this young woman?' Jock shouted at Cairn.

Unruffled, Cairn replied coldly, 'I was discussing business that is no business of yours, Jock.'

'Oh, so you remember my name, eh?' Jock snapped at him.

'You own the bar restaurant with Judy,' Cairn added, showing how much he remembered about all of them.

'Then you'll remember that I'm not the sort of man to put up with any nonsense from you or Sholto. So you can tell him that when he arrives.'

'I'll do that,' said Cairn. The coldness in his reply quelled the fiery tempers and prevented further heated discussions.

By now, Gordon had hurried round to the front of the shop, just in time to see Cairn leaving. They locked eyes, then Cairn walked away, got into his sleek car and drove off.

Everyone piled back into the tea shop, chattering, discussing what Eila had told them.

'I'll make fresh tea,' Gordon announced, rattling around behind the counter, still bristling with the thought that Cairn had wangled a dinner date with Eila.

Jock kept a protective arm around Judy's shoulders and sat beside her as they rejoined the other bee members.

'A dinner date tomorrow night with the blond fox?' Minnie sounded wary of Cairn's motives. 'He's a wily customer.'

'That was a stealthy move by Cairn,' Pearl added.

Minnie watched Gordon making the tea. The tension showed on his face. 'I think Gordon's upset that Cairn has asked Eila out before he had a chance to do it.'

The others agreed.

'It's just business,' Eila assured them.

'You sound less convinced than we are,' said Minnie.

'A dinner date with Cairn is playing with fire,' Jock warned Eila.

Eila didn't doubt it, but she was intrigued by his invitation.

Gordon overheard them as he brought the tea through. 'Are you definitely going to have dinner with Cairn?'

Eila looked up into Gordon's concerned eyes. 'Yes, he's picking me up at seven. I offered to drive up, but he insisted on coming to get me.'

'To make sure you go,' Jock said, suspicious of Cairn.

'I won't be compromised by him,' Eila told them. 'Or cajoled into doing anything I don't want.'

'I'll give you my number,' said Gordon. 'Phone if you want to cut your evening short and need a lift home. It's quite a walk, especially at night, through the trees.'

The others nodded, and several numbers and details were exchanged before they drank their tea.

'I'll get the chocolate cake and truffles,' Gordon said, trying to lighten the atmosphere.

Cairn sat outside Sholto's house on the patio drinking a cup of coffee. The patio doors from the main lounge were wide open, letting the warm air in. The sea breeze on the shore had a coolness to it, but up here, buffered by the thick trees and shrubbery, the air had some heat in it.

Cairn had taken his jacket and tie off and relaxed in his open neck white shirt. He still looked immaculate even when he wasn't buttoned up and dressed to impress. Had he impressed Eila? He didn't know. She'd certainly impressed him. He couldn't stop thinking about her.

He sipped his coffee and shrugged off the sense of her, the way she spoke to him, fiery yet polite, knowledgeable but willing to share that knowledge with him. His offer to pay her seemed to make her uncomfortable. In her world business was conducted for payment, but also included exchange of information for mutual benefit. She was right that some things benefited everyone, but he didn't live in that world. His was clear cut business, cut–throat some would say. He'd been called a shark in a suit a few times and didn't feel it unwarranted. But he'd no intention of using his skills to outmanoeuvre her. Besides, she may have a slight advantage over him. For the first time in a long while, he felt his heart melt a little when those eyes of hers looked at him, challenging him, urging him to be a better man.

Shrugging off the images of Eila openly showing him her notebooks, her plans, her contacts, he sipped his coffee and tried to concentrate on business. Sholto would be here the day after tomorrow. That gave him one day to work on business — and one night to have dinner alone with Eila.

Pearl was delighted with her fabric bundles, and other bee members were planning to pop into Eila's shop to buy some for their quilting.

As the ladies discussed fabric and embroidery thread with Eila, Gordon started to put everything away. He kept the tea shop tidy, and as the last of the ladies filtered out, Eila was left to pick up her sewing bag and get ready to leave. She paused to admire the vintage decor in the function room and felt the fresh breeze blow in through the patio doors. The scent of the garden merged with the sea air.

What a day it had been — an opening day to remember. And an unforgettable night. Images of Cairn's handsome face clashed with those of Gordon's warm smile and his lean but strong build striding out of the sea every morning. Even when the water looked wild with frothy crests rolling on to the shore, Gordon remained strong when the waves were against him. She liked Gordon. She'd liked him since the first time she'd seen him swimming, and she liked him even more when he'd brought her a cake and made her feel welcome.

'What a night!' Gordon's words jarred her from her thoughts. He leaned against the doorway between the function room and the tea shop and smiled at her.

'I was just thinking that.'

She shrugged her bag on to her shoulder and walked towards him.

'Is it always so chaotic living here?' she asked him lightly.

He nodded firmly. 'Better get used to it.'

'I'm tempted to retreat again into the cottage at the back of my shop and sew dresses while the world outside rages on.'

Gordon shook his head. 'Nooo, retreating isn't allowed. You'll have to forge ahead and deal with the daily drama and evening chaos.'

'You seem to thrive on it.'

'I suppose I do,' he mused. 'I probably add to the chaos sometimes.'

Eila smiled at him. 'On the surface you look calm, but underneath the water you're paddling like blazes.'

Gordon disagreed. 'It's the complete opposite. I'm a calm paddler. But on the surface I'm flapping like mad. I think there's a certain achievement in not disguising the chaos.'

They walked together through to the front of the tea shop. They were alone now and most things had been tidied away.

She gazed around at the beautiful decor. The amber and pink glow from the lamps created a cosy atmosphere, as did the lights from the display cabinets and counter. Outside the windows the sea glistened under a dark, stormy sky.

'It looks like a storm is on its way,' she said.

'I think it's arrived.'

She nodded. 'Cairn.'

'Yes.'

She sighed heavily.

'I know it's late, you must be exhausted from the hectic day, the crazy night, and need to get some sleep because you'll have to do it all again when you get up early tomorrow morning.' He paused then added, 'But...would you like a cup of tea before you go?'

She hesitated, then said, 'Yes. And could I have one of those tasty truffles?'

Gordon looked happy. 'Coming right up.'

Eila wandered around admiring everything. 'I love your tea shop, Gordon.'

'Thank you,' he called through to her from the kitchen. 'Do you like butterscotch or fudge?'

'Yes.'

He laughed, and she found herself starting to relax. Being in the tea shop at night with the storm raging outside, felt cosy. And she felt at ease with Gordon.

'Here you go.' He carried through a tray with tea and tasty sweets and set it down on a table at the window.

Eila sat down opposite him, gazing out at the sea while Gordon poured their tea and plied her with sweets.

She bit into a square of rich fudge and nodded at him. 'Your sweets are delicious. You're spoiling me.'

Gordon continued to spoil her until it was quite late.

'So you trained as a patisserie chef in Glasgow?' she said.

Gordon nodded. 'I also considered specialising in chocolatier work.'

'But now that you have the tea shop, you can make your own chocolates.'

'Exactly. My confectionery has become quite popular. I like to try new flavours.'

Gordon talked about his new truffles, Eila spoke about the new fabrics, but neither of them brought up the subject of Cairn, until it was time for Eila to leave.

'Thank you again for the tea and sweets.'

'Anytime, Eila. And I hope your dinner with Cairn goes well.'

She nodded, picked up her bag and headed towards the door. As Gordon opened it the wind blew in and the sound of the storm raged outside. They'd been so engrossed in each other, chatting over tea, that the storm had picked up pace.

'Let me grab my jacket. I'll walk you along to your shop.' Gordon ran upstairs to grab his jacket.

Eila shivered and wished she'd worn more than a blouse and skirt. But her shop was nearby, so she'd manage.

Gordon ran down wearing a dark leisure jacket and handed her a similar jacket with a hood.

'Put this on. It'll shield you until you get to the shop.'

He zipped her into the jacket and pulled up the hood. It was far too big for her, and she tried and failed not to laugh as Gordon adjusted the toggles and hood to make it fit.

'You're drowning in there,' he said, smiling.

'Did you say something? I couldn't hear you from inside this padded fortress.'

He laughed and tightened the hood. 'Grab a hold.' He held his arm out for her to hold on to. 'Anchor yourself down.'

Eila linked her arm through his and held on tight. 'Ready when you are.'

Gordon opened the door and struggled to stop it from banging off its hinges while keeping a grip on Eila. Locking it secure, he headed for the dress shop, shielding her with his manly stature against the elements.

Eila tucked into Gordon and hoped the gusts didn't blow her skirt up.

'Are we walking at a steep angle, or have I eaten too many sweets?' she shouted.

'Probably both. Hang on, we're almost there. Give me your key. I'll open the door.'

Snuggling into Gordon, she let him hustle her inside. He gave her the key, pulled the door shut and shouted through to her. 'Lock it and secure the windows.'

Eila locked the door and gave Gordon the thumbs up.

He waved and headed back to the tea shop.

Eila smiled as she unravelled herself from the voluminous jacket.

After a night as hectic as this, dinner with Cairn would be a skoosh.

CHAPTER SIX

Cairn closed the patio doors against the stormy night and went upstairs to his bedroom.

He showered and then padded through to the bedroom and got ready for bed. The silky pyjama pants he wore hung low on the lean muscles of his long torso, and his broad shoulders still felt the pressure of the day.

His blond hair looked a few shades darker, dripping wet, and he swept it back from his troubled brow as he gazed out the window at the trees being buffeted by the wind — and thought about Eila.

What did she think of him? And why did her good opinion of him matter?

All those familiar but disapproving faces looking at him in her shop showed quite clearly that their opinion of him wasn't of merit. If he'd cared enough this would've annoyed him. But he knew their resentment of him was too intense for them to view him fairly.

Whatever past slights or supposed indiscretions they blamed him for, he doubted the gulf would be breached amicably. It was better to get on with his business and let them do likewise. Some people would never be the best of friends.

Eila was ready for bed but was still buzzing from the events of the evening — including enjoying tea with Gordon. She supposed she should get some sleep and yet...

She poured herself a glass of milk and settled down in the cosy living room, checking her laptop for online orders. There were a few, and she'd deal with them in the morning.

The notebooks caught her attention, and she pulled them down from the shelf and decided to make a start on the lists she'd promised to give Cairn.

It didn't take long because she was so familiar with the fabric suppliers and knew exactly the contacts to give him. The list done, she then added some notes for reference, explaining her colour combinations and attached pictures of her choices.

By the time she'd finished she'd given him all the information he'd need, and it seemed reasonable to email it off to him rather than do it in the morning when she'd be busy with the shop. So she typed a message, attached the lists and images, and emailed it to the address he'd given her.

She sighed and smiled to herself. Job done, and finished her milk.

The storm continued to roar along the esplanade, sweeping in from the sea. But she felt safe and warm, tucked into the cottage at the back of the shop.

She'd been concerned that she'd miss the city, but she hadn't at all. The moment she'd stepped into the shop and the cottage she'd felt at home, as if the life she'd always dreamed of had been here all along. Now, she couldn't imagine going back to the city. This was where she belonged.

Deep in thought about the fun she'd had at the quilting bee, and Gordon's tea shop, she jolted when the email she'd sent to Cairn pinged a reply...

Cairn hadn't been able to settle, so he'd sat on the edge of his bed and checked his laptop for business emails. There was rarely any other kind.

That's when he'd seen the email from Eila pop up — at this time of night! He'd imagined she'd be tucked up in bed by now, sleeping sound. But no, there was her email with lists and other information attached. He'd skimmed through it, and then sent a quick reply in the hope that she was still online...

Eila read Cairn's email:

Thank you for sending me the lists of your suppliers, and including details of your fabric colours. I appreciate you taking the time to do this, and your generosity in sharing this with me.

Looking forward to chatting to you over dinner.

Best, Cairn.

Eila typed a speedy reply:

I hope you find the lists helpful. I couldn't sleep, and decided to put the lists and information together for you.

See you tomorrow night.

Eila.

She pressed the send button.

A few minutes later an email came back with attachments:

These are the types of suits and waistcoats that I think the new fabrics and the new colour combinations would be ideal for. Thought you might be interested in seeing them.

Sorry you couldn't sleep. I couldn't sleep either. Such a stormy night.

Eila read the message and then clicked on the attachments. There were pictures of stylish men wearing suits, standing in the heart of the city, Edinburgh. Clearly the pictures had been taken by a professional photographer for Sholto's company website or advertising features.

She enlarged a couple of the pictures and noted the exquisite details on the suits. The cut, the designs, the style — sheer class. If Sholto was aiming to outdo himself and up the level of the suits, he had a hard task ahead of him. So too, she thought, did Cairn and Sholto's sons.

Scrolling through the pictures she admired images taken in the snow, in the wilds of the Scottish Highlands, and recognised the man modelling the suits — Cairn.

Her heart squeezed just looking at him. Cairn was heartbreakingly gorgeous, and she lingered on these images, taking him in.

Her fingers flew over the keys to send a reply:

Great pics! You must've been freezing modelling those suits in all that snow. I didn't know you were a model.

She was teasing him, but pressed the send button and wondered what he'd say, if anything. Perhaps he'd gone to bed. How long had she lingered, admiring those pictures?

Moments later he replied:

Ha! Model indeed. Definitely not. I stepped in when the model we'd hired for the photo–shoot got cold feet, literally.

But I thank you for the compliment.

She responded:

I really do admire the suits. Traditional, classy. I'm not sure how you're going to outshine these designs. Some things are perfect as they are. New fabric would obviously help with your next collection, but I'd be wary to make something less than it might have been just because you think it needs changed. Subtle new colours, especially for the waistcoats and shirts, would obviously refresh the collection.

But it's a long time since I worked with my father. I did love tailoring. Love dressmaking more.

He replied:

It's always valuable to have another perspective in this line of work. So I thank you for your insight and will pass you helpful comments on to Sholto, Hamish and Fraser. And I agree with you — some things are perfect as they are.

He wanted to add that this applied to Eila, but he didn't risk overstepping the mark. Not yet, perhaps not at all. Their worlds were so far apart. He would return to Edinburgh after their sojourn to the seaside. He couldn't imagine cajoling Eila to go with him. To work with them in the city. Even if they paid her well, her new life by the sea was of more value.

Cairn sent his reply without any personal indulgence.

Eila read the message and wondered what Sholto's reaction would be. Would he scoff at the remarks from a little dressmaker? According to Minnie and the others, Sholto was a forceful man, not easily pleased. But Cairn seemed eager to pass her comments on, and she didn't have to deal with Sholto. Dinner with Cairn was all that was left to do.

She typed quickly:

I should get some sleep now. Early start.

Cairn's reply indicated he didn't want their emails to end, though he knew they both had to get some sleep:

I hope you got some sewing done at the quilting bee. Apologises again for whisking you away. Get some sleep. See you tomorrow night at seven.

Eila responded:

No sewing. Plenty of chatter (gossip), tea, chocolate cake, butterscotch, fudge and chocolate truffles. Still buzzing. Probably why I couldn't sleep. But off to bed now. Night.

Cairn read Eila's last message of the evening and reluctantly closed the laptop.

He lay in bed thinking about her, knowing he shouldn't, but couldn't help himself. No rest for the wicked, he thought, no rest for him tonight.

Eila flicked the lights off in the shop and the cottage, leaving only one small lamp glowing in the bedroom.

Snuggling under the duvet she listened to the sounds of the storm, feeling safe and cosy in her cottage.

She thought about Cairn, what she'd wear for their dinner date, a business dinner date she reminded herself. The pictures of Cairn dressed in immaculate suits in the snow covered Highlands were fresh in her thoughts. Great images that allowed her to linger and study the extent of his handsomeness, something she hadn't done when talking to him in person. Cairn had the type of looks that urged her to gaze at him, but their email exchanges let her get to know him better. And yet, would she ever really know a man like him? Despite her love of tailoring and past experience from what she'd learned from her father about suits, her world and Cairn's world were never going to merge easily.

As she thought about Cairn, her mind rewound her night with Gordon and a warm–hearted feeling made her smile. Romance wasn't on her agenda. It was important to establish her business.

Thinking of everything that had happened that night, she fell asleep picturing Gordon and the tea shop...

Gordon was in bed. His bedroom had a view of the sea, and he watched the waves sweep along the shore. The storms were never as fierce as they looked. Filled with bluster, they tended to refresh everything and he expected the morning to be bright and airy. He'd still go swimming. It would take a lot more than a swirly wind and frothy waves to stop his daily dip.

He'd flicked the television on and had watched another episode of a series he'd been enjoying. But his thoughts kept drifting to Eila and their tea and chat. He enjoyed her company and wished he'd asked her to have dinner with him. He believed her when she said her dinner with Cairn was business, not a date. But the look Cairn had given him earlier outside the dress shop. He'd seen that look before. The look of a jealous rival, unmistakable.

Cairn probably intended gleaning information from Eila. That would've been his original plan. But there was something about Eila that made Gordon warm to her, a strong attraction. He reckoned Cairn had been smitten by her as well.

Amid all the gossip at the quilting bee, none of the women, not even Minnie, had considered that Cairn might start to have real feelings for Eila. All they spoke about was Cairn's cold–hearted attitude, a heartbreaker.

Gordon relaxed in his bed and pondered the possibilities. What if Cairn was in jeopardy of falling for Eila? For he knew that he certainly was. Eila was beautiful, talented and warm–hearted. No wonder Cairn had iced him with a challenging glare.

He wished that Eila wasn't having dinner with Cairn. He sighed heavily. Without having her car to drive herself home, she was reliant on Cairn bringing her back. Or perhaps he'd planned to entice her to stay the night?

He sighed again, and tried to settle down to sleep.

Eila dug her swimsuit out from the depths of her wardrobe. Her one and only swimsuit. She used to enjoy swimming during day trips to the coast, but she hadn't done that in a long time.

The storm made her realise that the summer would be over in a few weeks time and if she wanted to go swimming while the sea wasn't freezing, she'd better get her suit on now.

She'd slept well, but woke early. If she went for a swim now, she'd be back soon for a shower and breakfast, and open her shop at the usual time.

Determined to give it a go, at least once, she put her turquoise blue suit on, popped a towel in a bag, wore a light wrap around skirt and pumps, and ventured down to the shore.

No one was around. She had it all to herself. The sea was quite calm considering the previous night's storm.

The air was fresh and there was a sense that it would be a warm, late summer day.

She kicked her pumps off, untied her skirt and left her bag on the sand near the esplanade wall.

The sea stretched for miles, a deep blue–green, like the colour of Gordon's eyes. Yes, he'd been in her thoughts again, especially as she wondered if he'd see her from his tea shop.

The water was warmer than she'd thought, refreshing, and she waded in becoming acclimatised to the temperature before diving in. It felt great. No wonder Gordon enjoyed swimming every day.

Gordon put his fresh fruit tarts in the display cabinet, and was about to add the cupcakes when he noticed someone swimming in the sea.

Someone was swimming this early?

He focussed on them, and noticed that it was a woman.

Then he gasped. It was Eila!

He sparked into action, checked that there were no cakes, scones or anything baking in the ovens. Flicked off the kettle that was on for a cup of tea, ran upstairs, jumped into his swimming trunks, grabbed a towel and raced down to the shore.

'Eila!' Gordon called to her. 'Wait for me!'

He dived into the sea and powered towards her.

She looked round hearing him call her name, and smiled when she saw him causing more froth than the waves in his haste.

He bobbed to the surface near her and smiled. 'You're swimming!'

'Yes. The water is quite warm.'

Gordon swam beside her, smiling.

She thought he looked so handsome. He had a great smile.

'We must be crazy,' she shouted. 'We're the only two fools swimming at this early hour.'

'This is early even for me.'

They continued to swim along the coast and then headed back towards the shore.

Eila hoped he didn't want to race her.

'Race you back,' he called to her, and then began powering ahead.

She tried to keep up, and came a close second to Gordon as he stood up and walked on to the sand.

The muscles in his strong back rippled as he walked on and shook his wet hair back. Up close, his lean physique sent her heart fluttering, and she tried not to stare.

He was polite enough not to stare at her in her swimsuit, but his eyes flicked glances at her, admiring her pert figure.

Eila wrapped her skirt around her waist and stepped into her pumps. Her blonde hair was dripping wet, and the sun had broken through the last of the cloud cover, highlighting the glistening beads of water on her hair and face.

For a moment, Gordon couldn't help himself. He gazed at her and felt himself fall in love with her a little more, a lot more.

'I didn't think you'd see me.' She towel dried herself lightly, and walked back up with Gordon to the esplanade.

‘I saw you from the tea shop window.’

They stood for a moment smiling at each other, both lingering, then Eila said, ‘I’d better get showered and ready for business.’

Gordon blinked out of the moment. ‘I should too.’

Eila walked back to her shop and Gordon headed in the opposite direction.

Once inside the tea shop, he realised he’d missed a chance to invite her to go swimming with him tomorrow morning. A refreshing swim in the sea after her dinner with Cairn.

Mentally kicking himself he hurried upstairs to shower and get dressed.

Eila’s dress shop was quite busy during the day. Several quilting bee women had popped in to buy fabric bundles, embroidery thread, dresses and skirts. The skirts were really popular and she planned to make more of these. Sewing a wrap around skirt was easier than making a tea dress, and as she’d sold the majority of her stock, she now had the task of stitching new items for customers.

Her cutting table and sewing machine were set up at the far end of the living room, and although the cosy lighting created a welcoming atmosphere, she also used a daylight bulb lamp at her sewing table.

The shop had room for storing fabric, hanging up dresses and skirts, and gave her plenty of extra space for working on her sewing.

The cottage had a second bedroom and she used it as a spare store room. Overall, she was happy with the property. In Glasgow she’d worked in her living room and the stock had spilled into her bedroom, occupying more space in her wardrobe than her own clothes. So it was wonderful to have an actual shop as well as selling her dresses and skirts online. There was room to breathe, while still feeling the cosiness of the cottage.

She’d always worked fast at cutting out her patterns. Smoothing the fabric, making sure she had the nap and any print properly aligned with the paper pattern pieces. Then she’d cut it with the precision she’d learned from her father, without fuss or faltering. It took a sure hand and professional scissors to cut each piece to perfection. After tacking the garments together, she’d stitch them using the sewing machine. She also had an overlocker to finish the raw edges of the seams.

Evenings were precious because she could get so much work done, stitching away into the night.

But tonight she wouldn't get any sewing done, so she worked hard throughout the day, between serving customers and packing up orders, to ensure she kept up with her busy schedule.

Cups of tea kept her going through the day, and she grabbed a salad and tomato sandwich for a quick lunch. Now as the daylight softened, fading over the sea, she closed the shop and started to get ready for her dinner date.

CHAPTER SEVEN

Cairn arrived on time. He drove up in his expensive silver car, parked outside the dress shop, got out and knocked on the door.

Eila welcomed him in. She wore one of her favourite tea dresses, a floral print. Her shoulder–length blonde hair was brushed smooth and silky, and her makeup was natural looking and emphasised her lovely skin and blue eyes.

Again, Cairn's stature and presence filled the shop, causing flutterings of excitement through her. His dark grey suit worn with a white shirt and grey silk tie was class personified. He smelled good too, and his well groomed appearance had notched up another level. He'd clearly made an extra effort to impress her. And it had worked. She could barely concentrate on checking she had everything she needed for checking out Cairn's handsomeness.

'Busy day?' He glanced around the shop, noticing that quite a few items had been sold.

'Yes, local customers, especially the quilting bee ladies, have bought up all my fabric bundles and lots of embroidery thread. I've had to reorder quite a bit of stock.'

He nodded, taking this in, while wandering over to the rolls of fabric on the shelves.

'I noticed you included other colours in the lists you gave me. Have you sold all of those?'

'No, I included extra colours that I'd love to have that I thought would be suitable for you,' she explained.

He frowned. 'Why don't you stock those extra colours? I thought they were excellent, especially those in the blue tones.'

She smiled and shrugged. 'I have to work to a budget. I select as many colours as is cost–effective.'

She sensed him wish he hadn't asked. 'Of course. Silly of me.'

'I do make a profit,' she was quick to add. 'It's just not viable to buy up all the lovely colours in the ranges I listed for you.'

'Your selection for the dress shop is great. I hope I haven't offended you.'

'Not at all.'

'Do you now have to start making lots of new dresses? You seem to have sold quite a few.'

'I've been cutting like crazy today, between serving customers. The skirts as well as the dresses have been popular. But the skirts are easier to finish in an evening. The dresses take a bit longer.'

He looked around. 'Do you cut the fabric in here?' He glanced at the counter.

'No, I've got my cutting table and sewing machine set up in the living room.'

He nodded, remembering seeing her sewing machine when she'd showed him her notebooks. He'd been too taken with the notebooks, and Eila, to notice the cutting table.

'I have a pile of pattern pieces cut and ready to machine.'

'Could you show me? I'm interested in your cutting methods.'

'Eh, yes.' She led him through to the living room.

Lamps created a warm ambiance, and she walked over to the cutting table where she'd been working.

'You certainly have been busy.' He gestured to one of the pattern pieces. 'May I have a look?'

'Yes, but be careful of the pins. I haven't tacked them yet.'

Cairn lifted one of the pattern pieces for a dress from the top of the pile. The paper pattern was still pinned to the fabric.

'That's for one of the classic tea dresses. I've been making them for years and I machine most of them, overlock the raw edges of the seams and depending on the style, I'll machine or hand stitch the hem.'

'The cutting is precise.' He lifted the gleaming pair of scissors that were sitting on the table. Other scissors hung from a small rack on the wall. The tools of her trade.

She smiled, pleased that he appreciated the process for her dressmaking.

'Do you use this sewing machine for all your dressmaking?' There was no malice in his tone. He simply wanted to understand why she only had one machine.

'At the moment, yes. The vintage model is just for display. I plan on buying another sewing machine for the shop.'

He didn't ask, not wanting to make her talk about having to budget again.

'I like this machine. I'll probably buy the latest version of it once I've settled in.'

'You seem to have settled in well.'

'I have. Though I've only just started to get to know the local people. Last night was my first evening at the quilting bee.'

This seemed to surprise him. 'I thought you'd been a member since you arrived here from Glasgow.'

'No, I've sort of hidden away, stitching, getting used to things here. But I do like living here, in the cottage, and having the shop.'

'You seem happy.'

'I am. It's hard work, long hours, but then it's the same as I was doing in my flat in the city. This is a far better place to call my home.'

He nodded and looked around the living room. 'It has a homely quality.'

'Do you have a house in Edinburgh?' she asked.

'Yes. A townhouse in the city. It's near the company, so handy for work.'

She pictured that it would be stylish, like Cairn, and perhaps not homely.

'It's home, but not homely,' he confessed. 'Not like this cottage.'

'I always wanted to live in a cottage by the sea. I even went swimming this morning.'

He smiled. 'Swimming?'

She nodded. 'I thought I'd better make the most of the summer mornings before the weather changes. I'm not sure I'll be one of those hardy types that swims in all weathers.'

'I used to enjoy swimming. Haven't much time for things like that these days.'

'All business and no fun.'

'Business can be fun, especially on evenings like this. Would you like to head up to the house for dinner?'

'I'll get my bag.'

Eila flicked the lamps off, put on a white cardigan, picked up her bag and accompanied Cairn out to the car.

The sea breeze blew through her hair as he held the car door open for her.

The excitement she felt sent her heart fluttering again, sitting beside Cairn, as he drove off.

Gordon saw them drive past the tea shop. He'd seen Cairn drive up to the dress shop and wondered what was taking them so long to leave. He chided himself for watching out the window. He'd closed his tea shop for the evening, and was alone in the premises. Usually he'd be in the kitchen baking cakes, but curiosity made him want to see them.

A stab of jealousy caused him to flinch when he saw Eila sitting in the passenger seat of Cairn's sleek, silver car.

Eila was chatting to Cairn and never noticed him watching out the tea shop window. She looked lovely. Eila always looked lovely, but she was particularly attractive this evening. He envied Cairn rotten, and was upset with himself for letting his feelings run riot. What if the business dinner became a dinner date as the evening wore on? He hated to admit it, but Eila and Cairn looked like a well–groomed couple. What if Eila suited Cairn? What if a hundred things happened that twisted his guts into a pretzel?

He was out of the shop and watching the car drive off down the esplanade until the tail lights disappeared into the distance.

He sighed, hung his head down, tried to shake the hurt from himself, and went back into the tea shop.

He locked the door, and trudged through to the kitchen.

Baking cakes always made him happy. He loved baking. But he sensed that no amount of Victoria sponge or fruit cake would lighten his heart tonight.

He'd hardly eaten anything all day, knowing that Cairn had wangled a date with her.

Sighing heavily, he added more raisins and cherries to his fruit cake mix. Even the aroma of the spices, dark sugar and black treacle failed to lighten his mood. He should've made his feelings for Eila known to her, taken a risk that he'd be rejected. But, no, he'd decided to take his time, do things properly, while Cairn stepped in and was now taking her to dinner.

He couldn't imagine what dinner would be, but it was a sure bet it would be impressive. Cairn probably couldn't cook for toffee. According to Minnie, he'd hired caterers to deal with the whole thing.

Gordon put his fruit cake in the oven, and tried not to think of Eila swimming in the sea with him. They'd had a happy time together.

He whisked his meringue mix until it was standing up in stiff peaks, and then piped it on to a baking tray.

Every oven in the kitchen was soon filled with some sort of cake. Even ones he'd had no intention of baking. But he'd have no problem tempting customers tomorrow with his surprise lemon drizzle cake.

While he waited for the timers to ping, he buttered a toasted crumpet and ate it while sipping a cup of tea.

Come on, he urged himself. Don't let yourself be beaten by a rich, successful and handsome rival.

He shook his head in dismay, then buttered another crumpet, and tried not to think what Cairn was up to with Eila.

The drive up to Sholto's house didn't take long, but within minutes of leaving the shore, they were heading into a wooded area, thick with trees. Now she understood why Gordon had offered to give her a lift home if things went awry with Cairn. It was feasible to walk the fairly short distance down to the seashore, but she wouldn't want to venture through the dark trees at night. Probably not even during the day.

Cairn spoke about their tailoring business, and asked more about her dressmaking. He was polite, interested in hearing the things she did, and soon they arrived outside Sholto's house. Minnie had described it as — big, and it was. A large mansion set in grounds with no other property near it.

It didn't look homely.

Lights were on in several windows on the ground and first floor. Wide steps led up to the entrance, and the doors were open in readiness for their arrival. A couple of staff stood waiting inside.

Cairn parked the car in the driveway, and they got out and walked towards the house.

Cairn escorted Eila inside, giving an acknowledging nod to the staff. This seemed to be a signal for dinner to be served.

'We're through here in the dining room.' Cairn led her through to a huge room with a long dining table in the middle. It was set with white linen and silverware. Chandeliers hung from the high ceiling, and the only warmth came from a fire burning in the ornate fireplace at the far side of the room. The decor was a mix of classic and modern, and if Cairn had hoped to impress her, he had.

'I thought we could have dinner and then I'll show you the sewing room where we work when we're here,' Cairn explained.

Catering staff began serving dinner while Cairn continued, 'This is where Sholto first created his original designs, the suits that set him on his tailoring success. His father was wealthy, and this house has been in Sholto's family for many years.'

'But he's based in Edinburgh and doesn't come here very often,' said Eila.

'He's rarely ever here, but he's reluctant to sell the house because it's his heritage.'

Eila was offered a choice of soup and selected Scottish vegetable, as did Cairn.

'It's a shame that a house like this isn't lived in,' Eila commented.

'Sholto keeps talking about leasing it out. Fraser also considered living here when he was training to be a chef. Sholto's ex–wife, Cynthia, owns a successful catering company and had high hopes that Fraser would join her, but both sons opted to work with Sholto.'

'You mentioned that Hamish and Fraser aren't keen to come here.'

'No, but we'll all make the most of it.' Cairn gestured around him. 'If I'd known I'd be dining with someone like you, I'd have looked forward it.'

Eila blushed and smiled. 'When do they arrive?'

'Lunchtime tomorrow.'

Eila ate her soup and wondered what type of trouble this would cause.

'Sholto would like to meet you.'

Eila blinked. 'Why?'

'I sent him the information you gave me. He was very impressed, and he'd like to talk to you while he's here.'

She pictured the reaction from Gordon, Minnie and the others when she told them this.

'You will of course be paid for your time,' Cairn added.

There he was again, adding money to the mix. It made her feel uncomfortable, though he didn't seem to sense this. He was probably so used to paying for what he wanted. She supposed it was better than being miserly and not paying people if they did any work for them. But she wasn't used to being part of this type of business world.

They chatted about fabric, the new tailoring collections and she found herself enjoying being with Cairn. There was a calmness about him, and despite his obvious good looks, she felt quite relaxed in his company. She hadn't expected this. Not at all.

She was offered roast chicken or fresh salmon, and chose the latter. It was served with roast potatoes and a medley of vegetables.

Again, Cairn opted for the same as Eila. She didn't think he was doing this deliberately. They simply had similar taste.

Gordon's ovens were pinging like crazy, but he handled them like a maestro. Cakes were checked, taken out of the oven, placed on cooling racks and left to settle.

Gordon himself was unsettled. Eila would be having dinner with Cairn by now. He'd be plying her with sweet treats and sweet talk. What chance did he have against a man like Cairn?

A call came through to him from Minnie.

'I wasn't going to phone, because I don't like interfering, but I wanted to check that you were okay,' she said.

'I'm glad you called. I've baked more cakes than I know what to do with.'

'Did you see Cairn driving off with Eila?'

'Yes.' His heart sank as he replayed watching her leave with Cairn.

'I happened to be looking out the window of my shop,' Minnie explained. 'I saw his car. Eila was wearing a nice white cardigan. I couldn't help but notice them.'

'I can't settle,' he confided. 'I keep thinking that I should've talked her out of going. Then I say that it's not my place. It's not as if I'm dating her.'

'We saw the two of you swimming this morning,' Minnie told him.

'Who saw us?' he asked.

'It would be easier to say who didn't see the pair of you cavorting in the froth.'

'There was no cavorting, Minnie.'

She giggled.

'Oh, that I wish there had been,' he said.

'You were racing each other,' Minnie reminded him. 'You should've let her win. She nearly beat you. Eila's got a strong competitive streak.'

He sighed, thinking Minnie was right. He shouldn't have tried too hard to win.

'Eila looked lovely in her turquoise swimsuit,' Minnie told him.

Gordon agreed. 'What do you think Cairn is doing now? I mean, is it just a business dinner? The more I think about it the less convinced I am. But maybe I'm just winding myself up.'

'We thought you might be,' said Minnie.

'What do you mean, we? Is there someone else with you at the shop?'

'Just Pearl and Judy. And Bracken. We were going to take him for a walk. Fancy coming with us?'

'Where are you going?' He sounded suspicious. 'You're up to something.'

'When are we ever not up to something?' She paused, then said, 'So, are you coming with us to Sholto's house?'

The sensible part of him wanted to say no. But he heard himself reply with glee. 'I'm on my way.'

Gordon threw his jacket on, left the cakes to cool, and ran along to Minnie's grocery shop.

Pearl, Judy and Minnie were waiting for him. Minnie had Bracken on the lead. The dog was happy to see Gordon and wagged his tail.

'Pile in,' said Judy, urging them to get into her car that was parked outside the shop.

'I thought you were taking Bracken for walkies,' said Gordon.

At the mention of walkies the dog barked and became quite skittish.

'Shhh!' Minnie scolded Gordon. 'Don't mention the W word.'

Minnie calmed Bracken down and they all piled into Judy's car.

'You haven't told me what you're planning,' Gordon said, climbing in the back seat, sandwiched between Pearl and Bracken.

Pearl dug out a pair of night sights from her knitting bag. She held them up triumphantly to Gordon.

He frowned. 'Binoculars?'

Pearl shook her head. 'No, these are Jock's night sights. Binoculars for seeing things in the dark.' She put them back in the bag.

'I'm surprised that Jock isn't clinging on to the roof of the car and coming with us,' Gordon said flippantly.

'Jock doesn't know I've snaffled his night sights,' Judy told him, as she drove them up into the wooden area.

'You know that we're on a hiding to nothing doing this,' said Gordon.

'It's better than sitting worrying about Eila and doing nothing,' Minnie replied. 'But we've no intention of going too near Sholto's house.'

'That's why we need the night sights,' said Judy.

Minnie told Gordon their plan. 'We're going to lay low, hide near the trees, and keep an eye on things from a distance. Those windows in the dining room haven't got the curtains up yet. Pearl was there today and made sure of it.'

'I insisted on taking them home to iron them,' said Pearl.

'So we'll be able to see Cairn and Eila having dinner in the dining room,' Judy explained.

Minnie nodded. 'And if we see any funny business going on, we'll be able to run and help Eila if Cairn pounces on her.'

Gordon's heart pounded. 'Do you think that's what he's planning?'

'When I was up there today, tidying a few things, titivating the sewing room, I heard Cairn on the phone to Sholto,' said Pearl. 'He was singing her praises. Cairn sounds like a man smitten with Eila. This is the only night he'll have the house to himself with her before Sholto and his sons arrive.'

Gordon's hopes that this was just a business dinner were fading fast.

'Cairn's cunning,' Minnie said, 'so it's up to us to outmanoeuvre him and keep Eila out of trouble.'

As Judy drove deeper into the trees, Gordon saw the lights of the house shining through the branches. A surge of excitement charged through him. Or perhaps it was trepidation. Either way, he was up for getting involved. The only thing he wondered about was — who was going to keep them out of trouble?

'Why do we need Bracken?' Gordon asked.

‘Because if our plan goes awry, we can say we were just out for a jaunt to take Bracken for his nightly walkies,’ said Minnie.

Bracken started to bark and jump around in the back seat of the car.

Gordon had a feeling that trouble was brewing.

CHAPTER EIGHT

Gordon and the ladies hid in the shadows of the trees. Minnie had Bracken on the lead, and he was happy to sniff around the grass.

Everyone was under strict instructions not to mention the W word. Stealth was necessary if they were to avoid being seen by Cairn.

They spoke in whispers.

The air was cool, but the trees provided adequate cover and shielded them from the light breeze.

Gordon breathed in the fresh night air, hoping it would steady his nerves. He hid at the side of a tree and had a good view of the house. At first, he didn't see anyone, only the lights on in various rooms on the ground floor.

'There they are.' Minnie pointed to the dining room. It was all lit up and they had a clear view of Eila and Cairn having dinner.

Pearl had the night–sights and adjusted the focus as she peered over at them.

'They're at the pudding stage.' Pearl relayed the details. 'Eila's having whipped cream something or other. I'm not sure what Cairn is eating.' She thrust the night–sights at Gordon. 'You're the expert. Have a look.'

Gordon peered through night–sights. 'These night binoculars are really great. I can even see Eila's cherries. The details are amazing.'

'What is she having?' Minnie wanted to know.

'An ice cream sundae with whipped cream and cherries on top,' said Gordon. He then focussed on Cairn. 'He's spooning up what looks like sticky toffee pudding. I'm not sure if he's enjoying it, because he keeps looking at Eila.'

Gordon handed the night–sights to Minnie.

Minnie took a peek and sounded perturbed. 'Eila doesn't even know he's ogling her.' She passed the night–sights to Judy.

'I wouldn't say Cairn is ogling her,' said Judy. 'He seems quite smitten with her.'

Minnie reassessed her comment. 'Yes, you're right. He looks very taken with Eila.'

None of these comments bolstered Gordon, and he felt himself become deflated.

'Are you okay, Gordon?' Pearl asked.

'I'm...I'm just...' Gordon sighed in frustration. 'I just wish I'd asked Eila to have dinner with me. But as always, I'm pipped at the post.'

Minnie saw the discontent on Gordon's face as he stared across at the dining room. 'Remember, we're in stealth mode. So even if you feel like running over and causing a scene, keep a lid on it.'

Gordon nodded. 'I won't do anything wild and careless.'

Judy smiled. 'No, leave that up to us.'

Minnie pursed her lips at Judy. 'We all agreed to behave ourselves.'

Pearl scoffed. 'When did that ever stop us from causing chaos?'

No one had a suitable answer.

They continued to watch Eila and Cairn finishing their puddings. Eila seemed to be enjoying her sundae.

Bracken had settled down on the grass, happy to be where he was with Minnie.

'They're going through to the lounge now to have their tea,' said Pearl, viewing them through the night–sights. 'Cairn's opening the patio doors and they're stepping outside to get some air.'

'Hide in case they see us,' Minnie urged them.

All of them pressed themselves into the shadows of the trees.

'Eila's wearing a lovely tea dress,' Pearl commented. 'Now she's taking her cardigan off.'

Gordon took control of the night–sights. 'What's she doing? Cairn is moving in on her, he's too close and he's peering at her—'

Minnie interrupted. 'Ah, she's showing him the stitching on her dress. They must be talking about sewing.'

Gordon relaxed a little. 'Eila does look nice, doesn't she?'

'She certainly does,' Minnie agreed.

The others nodded.

Minnie gasped. 'Oh look, he's fiddling with her inner seams.'

Judy praised Eila's skill. 'Eila finishes her raw edges beautifully. It's put me in the notion of getting an overlocker machine.'

Gordon felt like someone was throwing him around, causing his heart to bounce in his chest, first one way, then the other.

'The stitching on her dresses is lovely,' said Pearl. 'No wonder Cairn is interested.'

Gordon looked away. 'I don't think I can watch any more of this.'

Pearl took the night–sights off him. 'Cairn seems to be gleaning a lot of information from Eila. Now he's digging into his trouser pocket and pulling out his...'

Gordon sounded anxious. 'Pulling out his what?' He urged Pearl to tell him.

'His phone,' said Pearl. 'He's phoning someone. Probably Sholto.'

There was a moment's lull, and then Pearl jumped when her phone rang, lighting up her skirt pocket and playing a lively and rather loud ringtone.

The sound attracted Cairn's attention, and he looked over towards the ringing.

'Answer it,' Minnie urged Pearl, grabbing the night–sights off her so Pearl could fish her phone out.

Pearl clicked the button and tried to sound relaxed, as if she was cosy at home, instead of prowling around in Cairn's bushes.

'Hello, Cairn,' said Pearl. 'What can I do for you?'

The others stared at Pearl wondering why Cairn had phoned her. They all kept quiet while she spoke to him.

'The keys to the sewing room? Yes, I know where they are,' said Pearl. 'I gave your drawers a good polish this morning. You'll find the keys in the dresser dookit in the kitchen. That's right. Yes, I'll hold while you go and look for them.'

Pearl whispered urgently to Minnie and the others. 'He wants to know where the keys to the sewing room are. Apparently, the evening staff don't know.'

'He'll be giving Eila a tour of the room,' Judy surmised.

'What's in it?' Gordon was eager to know.

'Fabric galore,' Pearl enthused. 'The shelves are filled with it. Expensive fabric for suiting. Sholto and the others work in there when they're staying here.'

'I've been in it,' Minnie revealed. 'Pearl had to prise me away. I could've spent all afternoon in it.'

Pearl grinned. 'I gave Minnie a wee peek one day when no one was at home. Cairn will be hoping to impress Eila.'

Minnie nodded. 'Eila's like us, she loves fabric. She'll love having a feel at his textiles.'

Gordon sighed heavily. 'Will we be able to watch what they're up to in the sewing room?'

Pearl shook her head. 'No, it's situated in the heart of the house. It doesn't even have a window so that the light doesn't fade the material.'

'So he's taking Eila into a fortress of fabric?' Gordon sounded peeved.

The women nodded.

'There's everything from bolts of fine worsted wool fabric, cotton and linen, to georgette and satin,' Pearl explained.

Gordon ran his hands through his hair. 'We'll have to do something. He'll ply her with patterns as well.'

Cairn's voice was heard on the phone again to Pearl. She listened and then said to him, 'I knew that's where the keys were.'

'Say something to put him off,' Gordon hissed at Pearl.

'Did someone hiss at you?' Cairn asked her, suddenly suspicious.

'I've got the telly on,' Pearl fibbed. 'I'm watching a film while I stitch my quilting.'

'Sorry to disturb your evening, Pearl,' Cairn apologised. 'I'll let you get back to watching your film. Good–night.'

Cairn hung up.

Pearl clicked her phone off and put it back in her pocket. 'He's gone. We can talk now.'

Bracken had fallen asleep and was snoring in the grass.

'They're back on the patio,' Minnie observed. 'Eila's buttoning up her cardigan. Cairn's gesturing for them to go for an evening stroll.'

For a few minutes they watched Eila and Cairn walk casually out into the garden. They were chatting animatedly.

'Can you hear what they're saying?' Gordon whispered. 'I'm not familiar with sewing chat. You can probably get the drift of the conversation.'

Judy was the first to reply. 'I heard Cairn mention classic men's trench coats.'

'Do they make coats?' Gordon thought they only made suits, possibly waistcoats and maybe shirts and ties.

Pearl nodded. 'Their coats are gorgeous. Class personified.'

'They're walking over here!' Gordon whispered.

Bracken's floppy ears perked up at the W word and he barked with enthusiasm.

Minnie hushed Bracken, but the barking noises had sounded shrill in the night air.

'Cairn's looking straight over here at us!' Pearl gasped.

'Dive for cover, Pearl,' Minnie instructed her. Then she said to Gordon. 'Even if you have to reveal yourself, we must make sure he doesn't see Pearl, because it could affect her working for him.'

Gordon had no intention of revealing himself, and ducked behind a tree, as did Minnie and Judy.

However, Cairn had seen Minnie and was marching through the grass towards her.

Pearl lay face down in the long grass. She was thankful that Euan hadn't cut the grass yet or she'd have been seen for sure on a well manicured lawn.

'Come on, Judy,' Minnie urged her. She held tight to the lead as they walked with Bracken towards Cairn.

Gordon hid out of view and watched Minnie and Judy pretending to walk the dog.

'What are you doing here?' Cairn stared at Minnie and Judy.

The dog wagged his tail at Cairn, but Minnie pulled him to heel. 'Don't go scurrying around Cairn, Bracken. We don't want to mess up his nice suit.'

Judy spoke up. 'We're walking Minnie's dog, Bracken. He ran off when he saw a rabbit. We've only just caught him.'

'He's on the lead now,' Minnie assured Cairn.

Judy and Minnie smiled brightly as if nothing was untoward.

'But it's dark out there. What are you doing prowling around the property?' Cairn wanted an explanation.

So Minnie gave him one. 'Judy often likes to accompany me when I take Bracken for a jaunt at night. We're so used to the house being empty. We were busy talking and enjoying our stroll, and forgot that you were here now. But don't worry. We'll not be venturing this way until you and Sholto have faffed off back to Edinburgh.'

Cairn frowned, taken aback that they were lurking in the shadows, and that they had a dog with them. The dog sealed the deal.

He believed them. They were silly enough to go for a walk in the wilds. Nothing about these ladies would surprise him, he thought, but finding them in the garden had taken him aback.

Eila had now joined him, and she'd heard the conversation.

Minnie and Judy smiled tightly, encouraging Eila to go along with the ruse.

Eila pretended not to be surprised and smiled sweetly, then she froze when she saw Gordon peering at her from behind a tree. He signalled for her to keep quiet about him being there. She nodded surreptitiously.

Then Eila blinked when she noticed Pearl lying face down in the long grass. Cairn was about to walk towards Pearl's hiding place.

Eila shivered in an exaggerated manner. 'Would you mind if we went back inside, Cairn? This dress isn't warm enough for a chilly evening. She wasn't wearing her cardigan, and did look a bit cold, though it was more from the surprise at seeing Gordon and the ladies.

Cairn swept Eila inside immediately. 'Yes, of course. Let's go in and I'll show you the sewing room. It's cosy in there.'

Gordon snarled to himself. Cosy indeed. Yes, he bet it was.

As Eila walked back to the house, she glanced over her shoulder. She saw Minnie and Judy walk away into the trees. Minnie waved, and she saw Bracken's tail wagging happily. Along with them Gordon trudged through the greenery. He gazed longingly at Eila.

For a moment Gordon and Eila looked at each other, and then Eila went into the house with Cairn.

Gordon and the ladies piled into Judy's car. Bracken sat in the back seat again with Gordon and Pearl.

The car had been hidden in the depths of the trees.

They chatted as Judy drove them back down to the shore.

'Cairn looked very handsome,' Minnie remarked. 'I think he'd made an extra effort to impress Eila.'

'He smelled lovely too,' Judy added. 'And I bet if Eila kissed him he'd taste of toffee.'

Gordon was uneasy at the thought of Eila kissing Cairn.

'I don't think she'll kiss him,' Judy was quick to add, glancing at Gordon in the rearview mirror.

'I'm glad Cairn didn't see me hiding in the grass.' Pearl sounded relieved. 'Thankfully, Eila distracted him.' She sighed. 'We get ourselves into some pickles!'

As they arrived back at the shore, Judy stopped the car outside Gordon's tea shop.

'Come on in for a cuppa and cake,' Gordon offered, unlocking the door.

Judy and Pearl followed him in. Minnie took Bracken to the grocery shop before joining them.

'The tea shop smells delicious,' Minnie said, sitting down at one of the tables while Gordon served up the tea.

'I was baking like a man possessed,' Gordon explained. 'I'd no intention of baking a lemon drizzle cake or extra chocolate cakes.' He served up the surplus cake with their tea.

'Thank you, Gordon,' said Minnie.

Judy and Pearl smiled too.

Gordon sighed and sipped his tea. He was inwardly torturing himself picturing Eila enjoying herself with Cairn in the sewing room.

The sewing room was beautifully lit, stocked with fabric, stacked on shelves, bolts of it in every subtle tone of grey and beige to autumn hues encompassing burnt ochre, chestnut, cinnamon and copper.

The dark tones ranged from slate and charcoal, into navy and deep sea blues that looked like they'd been inspired by the depths of the ocean.

'Sholto has an artist's eye for colour,' Cairn explained, showing Eila round the large room that was dominated by the cutting tables.

'He's an artist?'

'As a young man he enjoyed and had a talent for painting. But he always liked to dress well, and found he had an aptitude for designing suits. He sketched his own designs then made precision patterns. He initially had tailors sew the suits, though he selected his own fabrics. Then he trained in bespoke tailoring work and found his niche.'

'Did he start his business from this house?' she asked.

'He did, inspired he said by the colours and textures of the sea, the wild Scottish atmosphere of the day and evenings, and the distinct seasons. His first collection was entirely derived from those sources for the colours, patterns and style.'

'Now he wants to come back to where it all started?'

Cairn nodded.

'Will Sholto and his sons become involved in the local community?' she said, hoping to glean some details to pass on to Minnie and others. Obviously, from the antics earlier, they were concerned what was happening during her dinner with Cairn. They were also expecting Sholto to upset the equilibrium of the local people.

'No, Sholto will spend most of his time here, at the house, in the nearby wood, and go down to the shore without disturbing anyone. He used to enjoy walking along the esplanade, taking in the fresh sea air.'

'I'll probably see him,' said Eila. 'Though I don't know what he looks like.'

Cairn pointed to framed photos on the far wall of the sewing room. 'That's Sholto, Hamish and Fraser at one of their events to launch a new collection of suits.'

Eila went over and studied the men. Sholto was as she'd imagined — an immaculate and imposing figure. He looked like money. Cairn was standing beside him. 'You look so serious,' she chided him with a smile.

He smiled and felt the warmth of kindness from her.

'You should smile more,' she told him.

'I'll try,' he promised.

She looked again at the men. 'Which one is Hamish?'

'The sturdier of the two.'

'Hamish looks like his father.'

'He does. Sholto and Hamish share the same taste in tailoring.'

She thought Fraser was as tall, but leaner, a lighter but stylish version of them. She looked at Cairn and thought that he was a man in his own right. He fitted in with Sholto's sons, and arguably could've been seen as one of them.

He sensed her studying him.

'People often mistake me for being one of Sholto's sons. I've long felt part of the family.'

'It's great to have a strong bond in work and friendship in business,' she said, smiling at him.

Cairn couldn't remember the last time anyone spoke to him like this, with genuine interest. Lost in thought for a moment, he forgot to smile.

'You're looking serious again,' she reminded him cheerfully, and then went over to admire the sewing machines.

Four sewing machines of every top make that Eila recognised, were sitting along one side on vintage wooden tables equipped with thread racks and drawers. Everything had a place, and the efficiency was evident.

Scissors, cutting tools, rulers and other accoutrements of the trade were hung within handy reach, all gleaming new or vintage polished to shiny perfection.

Eila loved the room and wished she could wander around without feeling flustered when Cairn stepped closer to her than her heart could stand. He wasn't encroaching on her space, rather he was keen to show her the fascinating details of this marvellous room.

'We have a room like this in Edinburgh,' Cairn told her. 'But I'm inclined to think this was has an edge of class that appeals to my love of classic styling.'

'It's a beautiful room,' Eila enthused, gazing around.

Her hair shone under the spotlights, and Cairn found himself constantly distracted by her loveliness. But he didn't make any move to embarrass her. He could see that she was as taken with the sewing room as he'd always been. Adding romance to the mix would've jeopardised his original intention. He'd wanted to impress her, and by doing so, encourage her to see his world as he did, and perhaps with a fresh eye she could envisage new ideas that would be of help to their business.

He'd always thought he was a good judge of character, and he'd sensed Eila's true love of dressmaking, creating garments cut with precision, using fabric that leaned towards the classical end of the design scale. And yet, she was a modern woman, adventurous enough to forge a new life for herself here without the backing of anyone. That took guts, especially in today's world, when setting up a new shop in an untried location required great confidence. He admired her looks, but he truly admired her character.

Here she was, standing here, with no real benefit to herself, taking an interest in the business, and offering her opinion, something they rarely encouraged. Sholto had his own strong opinion on everything, but at their recent meeting he'd stated that he wanted to widen his views. When Cairn had phoned to tell him of Eila's fabric lists, Sholto surprised him with his eagerness to meet with her.

'Sholto, Hamish and Fraser will be here tomorrow,' said Cairn. 'But perhaps you'd be able to come back one evening next week to meet them for a chat.'

Wide blue eyes glazed up at him, and she smiled. 'Yes, I will.'

Cairn saw the clearest blue eyes he'd seen in years, and it disturbed him that he would do anything to betray the trust Eila had in him. He was determined to be upfront with her, disguising only his feelings for her. For now.

CHAPTER NINE

Minnie, Judy and Pearl were leaving the tea shop. Gordon glanced along towards Eila's shop.

'Eila will probably be back late,' Minnie said to him. 'She'll be engrossed in the sewing room.'

Pearl nodded. 'Yes, I wouldn't expect her back any time soon. You should get some rest, Gordon.'

Judy smiled at him. 'Thanks for the tea and cake.' She gave his arm a comforting squeeze. 'Don't worry about her. Everything will be fine.'

Gordon forced a smile.

'Sholto is arriving tomorrow with Hamish and Fraser,' Minnie said to him. 'Once Sholto gets here, Cairn will be too busy to have time for Eila.'

'You think so?' Gordon asked hopefully.

'Yes, Cairn will become involved in whatever Sholto and his sons are planning. When they've been here before, they hardly ever ventured down to the shore. They tend to keep to themselves in the house.'

'They always bring a disruptive element with them,' Judy added.

'So they won't be popping into my tea shop,' Gordon said, trying to make light of things.

'Nooo,' Minnie emphasised. 'Or my grocery shop. They hire staff to deal with their catering needs.'

Gordon was cheered by the thought that Cairn's time would be taken up with Sholto.

'Get some sleep, Gordon,' Judy advised him.

'Yes,' said Minnie. 'And when you wake up, make sure you do some of those things you wished you'd done regarding Eila.'

Waving to Gordon and each other, Minnie and Pearl headed home, and Judy went into the bar restaurant.

Judy had Jock's night–sights with her and planned to slip them back in his drawers. Maybe one day she'd tell him about their excursion up to the house, but at the moment Jock was still easily made jealous of her being near Cairn. She'd keep the night's adventure to herself.

Eila enjoyed using the sewing machines, and working with the various fabrics that Cairn suggested.

'This is a great machine,' she commented. It was far too expensive for her current budget, but she liked the way it stitched even the heavier worsted fabric easily. 'I love my sewing machine, and I'm used to its foibles, but it's nice to try new models like these.'

Cairn had set up all the machines, and showed her different finishes on fabric samples.

'I really should be going. It's very late, and I'm up in the morning.' She pried herself out of the sewing room.

'Thank you for having dinner and sharing your notes with me, Eila.'

Cairn walked with her to the car, and drove her down to the shore. They continued to chat about suits and sewing during the short drive.

Eila noticed the tea shop was in darkness, closed for the night, as they drove past. Only a dim light glowed in one of the windows upstairs, and she was surprised at her heart's reaction when she thought about Gordon.

Shrugging off the feeling, she got out of the car outside her shop.

Cairn walked her to the door. 'I won't come in. I've taken up enough of your time.'

'I had a lovely evening, Cairn.' She smiled at him.

'So did I.'

Cairn hesitated, and for a moment she thought he was going to kiss her goodnight, but stopped himself.

She went inside the shop and waved as he drove away.

Shrugging off her cardigan, and the effects of her evening with Cairn, she got ready for bed.

Lying in bed, gazing out at the night, she planned her day. She'd skip swimming in the morning and get on with sewing the new dresses and skirts.

She then fell asleep smiling to herself thinking about Gordon and the ladies prowling around Sholto's house, no doubt up to mischief.

Eila's morning was going to plan. She'd had porridge with creamy milk for breakfast, then started sewing, as she had done many mornings in Glasgow. She could get a lot done if she put her mind to it, didn't faff, or become distracted checking things online.

Unfortunately, something did distract her when she went through to the shop for extra thread for her sewing machine. Glancing out the window she noticed two men swimming in the sea. One of them had blond hair and the other's hair was darker.

She blinked, wondering if Gordon and Cairn had become friends? But then she saw Gordon walking down to the sea carrying his towel.

She focused on the figures swimming and was pretty sure one of them was Cairn. Yes, she could see him clearly now that he'd stood up in the water. It was definitely Cairn, but she didn't recognise the second man. Then it dawned on her that is was one of the men in the photo she'd seen in the sewing room — Fraser. He was handsome even from this distance, and had a lean, fit physique.

But it was Cairn's build she couldn't help but admire. His broad shoulders tapered down to a long, lean waist, lithe thighs and a pert—

Stop it! She scolded herself and blushed, even though the shop wasn't even open yet and there was no one there to see her.

Gordon walked down to the water as Cairn and Fraser stood in the shallows chatting.

Cairn nodded politely to Gordon.

Gordon nodded acknowledgement, and then dived into the sea.

'That's Eila's shop over there,' Cairn said to Fraser, pointing towards it.

'What's she like?' Fraser asked.

They stood for a moment looking over at the dress shop.

'She's very nice. Pleasant company. Knowledgeable about fabric, designs, colour combinations, patterns. Makes her own dresses.'

'How much are you paying her for her lists of suppliers and information?' Fraser asked.

'I offered an initial payment, and then I've offered her more money for all the extra information she was happy to give me during dinner last night,' said Cairn. 'But she told me she doesn't feel comfortable with me constantly offering to pay her for her help.'

'Really?' Fraser sounded surprised.

'Yes, but I won't take her assistance for our benefit without compensating her,' Cairn said firmly.

Fraser smiled. 'You like her, don't you? I can't remember you ever being quite so...*taken* with someone.'

'I'm not the only one,' Cairn admitted.

Cairn glanced over his shoulder and saw Gordon powering away along the coast.

'Who's the froth causer?' Fraser asked lightly. 'Is he annoyed with us? Or perhaps with you?'

Cairn explained about the dinner with Eila.

'I'm sure your dinner date didn't make Gordon's night,' said Fraser. 'What does he do? He looked quite fit. Is he one of the farmers?'

'No, he owns the tea shop.' Cairn indicated towards it.

'Nice shop. Very traditional style. I like that. I might even pop in there for afternoon tea.'

'I wasn't expecting you until lunchtime,' Cairn told him.

'My father and Hamish were arguing about stuff late last night. Usually they agree about new designs, but I think Hamish is annoyed at having to leave the city. So, rather than listen to a repeat of that this morning, I left before the dawn and drove straight here.'

'I certainly didn't want to come here,' Cairn confessed. 'But now I think it's quite a good idea to get away from the city for a while. Let's see what new designs we can come up with.'

Fraser paused and looked around. He took a deep breath of fresh sea air. 'I'd forgotten how invigorating the sea is,' he said, sweeping his light brown hair back from his brow.

Cairn sighed heavily. 'It is. I'll probably have just become accustomed to it when we have to leave.'

'Isn't that always the way of things.'

'It is. But for the moment, will we give the frantic frother a run for his money?'

Fraser exchanged a willing smile with Cairn. 'Oh, yes.'

Eila's heart lurched when she saw Cairn and Fraser dive into the sea again and power in the direction of Gordon. What were they up to? She thought they'd finished swimming. Now it looked like they were giving chase to Gordon.

She wondered what to do.

For a moment she thought she should mind her own business, stop being distracted, especially by handsome men tempting her with their toned bodies.

But what if Gordon needed back–up? It was two against one. She didn't think for one moment that Cairn was up to anything nasty, but the three of them in the sea was surely going to end in chaos.

Deciding to go and add to that chaos, Eila put her swim suit on and ran down to the sea.

The three men were way along the shore, but they'd have to head back soon. And when they did, she'd meet them face on.

Eila dived into the sea, wondering why this suddenly didn't seem like a great idea. But the sea felt fresh and she was determined now that she was there to give Gordon her back–up.

Jock peered out the window of the bar restaurant. He was wearing his kilt and had been up early to practice a tricky new reel for his ceilidh night. It was one of those fast–moving reels with spins and fancy footwork thrown in. He'd mastered it, but he needed to practise. This was the only chance he'd get because the ceilidh night started at seven, and he was busy in the bar and restaurant all day.

'Would you look at that!' Jock sounded displeased.

Judy was preparing a big pot of lentil soup for the bar lunches. She came hurrying over to the window. 'What is it?'

'Cairn and Fraser are sharking after our poor Gordon.'

Judy peered at the three figures in the water. 'Are you sure that's Cairn and Fraser? Fraser's not due until later.'

'I watched them standing nattering. It was definitely them. I'd recognise those two anywhere. You don't see many like them around here. Even their swimming trunks are tailored.'

'Oh, don't be silly, Jock,' Judy scolded him for exaggerating.

'Well...' he huffed. 'They're expensive looking swimming breeks that's for sure.'

Judy evaluated the situation. 'I don't think they're sharking after Gordon. They're all just swimming in the same direction.'

'I saw those scunners look at where Gordon was heading, and then they dived in and flailed like blazes after him,' Jock argued.

Judy was starting to believe Jock.

'I'm sure Gordon can take care of himself,' she said, hoping to calm him down.

But Jock had run off to the bedroom, whipped off his kilt, jumped into his baggy swimming trunks and galloped out the front door.

'No, Jock, no...' Judy shouted after him. 'Don't go causing trouble.'

'I'm going to stop any trouble,' Jock shouted back at her, and continued to power down to the shore in his bare feet.

Judy clutched at her blouse, worried that Jock would cause a rammy at sea. She squinted against the morning sunlight that was shining off the surface of the water. That's when she noticed someone else was in there swimming.

'Eila!' Judy gasped.

Judy's phone rang. It was Minnie.

'Have you seen the circus in the sea?' Minnie sounded distressed as she stood outside her grocery shop.

'I couldn't stop Jock,' Judy explained. 'He was worried that Cairn and Fraser had Gordon outnumbered.'

'But now Eila is swimming about in the surf with them! We have to do something. There could be a stooshie in the sea!'

Minnie's tone caused alarm bells to jolt Judy into action.

'You're right, Minnie. I'm going in after them. I swim like a fish. They won't sink me!'

'No, Judy. That's not what I had in mind,' Minnie shouted down the phone.

But Judy had clicked the call off and was now racing towards the sea, fully clothed.

Minnie frowned and shook her head. Judy's nice silk blouse of would be ruined in the salt water. And her new blonde highlights could turn green.

Minnie held her breath as she watched Judy cast her phone down on the sand, take a run at the water and power dive into the surf. She had no worries for Judy's safety, because Judy could swim like a barracuda and was fast catching up with them. It was the trouble she'd create as she overtook them — and the waves that Jock's anger would cause.

Six bedraggled figures finally traipsed out of the sea.

Minnie sighed with relief.

Jock had his arm around Judy, looking proud of her aquatic prowess — and although Judy's clothes were soaked, there wasn't a hint of green in her lovely blonde hair.

Eila looked distressed as she walked out of the shallows on to the shore. She was flanked by Gordon and Cairn.

Fraser was at the tail end of all the trouble and seemed a bit deflated.

Minnie pursed her lips in disapproval at Cairn and Fraser. She buttoned up her cardigan against the sea breeze. Another storm was brewing. Two more troublemakers were due to arrive soon. Sholto and Hamish were sure to add to the chaos.

Apart from thrashing around in the water, no one was jostled or in jeopardy. Only their egos were dented or silly intentions thwarted.

Judy and Jock headed back to their bar restaurant. Jock still had his arm around Judy and they were chatting animatedly about their impromptu swim.

Cairn and Fraser stopped at the two public shower stands to wash the sea water and sand from themselves while Eila and Gordon walked ahead and then paused.

'Are you okay, Eila?' Gordon asked, looking at her. Beads of water dripped from his hair and he wiped them away from his caring blue eyes. The tight grip he had on his rolled up towel showed the tension in him. His hand clenched it firmly. Adrenalin was pumping through his entire body from the exertion, rage and resentment. But none of this was directed at Eila. He'd wanted to protect her when he saw Cairn and the others in the sea close by. He thought he had, even though Eila was capable of looking after herself. She'd come to his rescue, aiming to back him up against Cairn and Fraser.

Gordon shook the water from his body along with the overwhelming urge to protect Eila, whatever way was necessary. To shield her from Cairn encroaching on her. To ensure Fraser didn't step in to cause her concern. Eila stood there in her turquoise swim suit looking beautiful and yet vulnerable. She wasn't even wearing any shoes. He wanted to lift her up in his arms and carry her safely to her shop, but he knew he shouldn't. Eila didn't need his help. As vulnerable as she appeared, she was a strong and independent young woman. But that didn't stop him feeling protective of her. All these thoughts were there and gone in a moment, and in that time Eila had looked at him and smiled.

'I'd no intention of going swimming this morning,' Eila told Gordon. 'But I thought there was going to be trouble.'

Cairn and Fraser stood side by side at the open shower stands and let the clean water rinse the salt and sand away.

Cairn's taut torso glistened in the sunlight as the water washed over him.

Fraser did the same, showering the sea water from his lean physique.

They were comparable in height. Both handsome men with fit builds.

Minnie stood outside her shop and spoke to Pearl.

'They're beautiful men, that's for sure, but Gordon holds up strong and handsome in his own way,' Minnie commented.

'He does,' said Pearl. 'So now we've got Cairn and Fraser for our entertainment. I hope they're not going to give us a show every morning while they're here. If they do, there will be a throng of women on the esplanade watching them.'

'I won't be one of them,' Minnie said, turning her back on them and going inside her shop. Pearl followed her in.

Fraser ran his hands through his hair, letting the water rinse it clean. The muscles in his arms flexed with every movement.

Even without their suits, Cairn and Fraser looked like money.

Cairn felt a pang of envy seeing Gordon standing chatting to Eila, but he didn't intervene. He'd done enough this morning by challenging Gordon to a swimming race. No one knew if either of them won in the meleé.

'We haven't been swimming since our trip to the South of France last year,' Fraser remarked while standing under the shower. Fraser's face was handsome, with an elegance in his looks and manner, but without the sheer beauty of Cairn. He'd inherited his pale grey eyes from his father, and his fine features from his mother.

'That's right,' Cairn agreed, remembering the trip. It had involved their company designing suits for several actors, including the leads, in a prestigious movie.

Fraser cast a glance around the Scottish shore. 'There's not much difference between the locations.' Fraser's comparison remark was steeped in sarcasm. Fraser obviously preferred the former.

'I prefer it here,' said Cairn. He watched Eila walking away to her shop. He couldn't help but admire her lovely figure.

Fraser followed the line of Cairn's distracted vision and smiled. 'I suppose you think the view is better from here.'

Cairn cast Fraser a look. 'I don't intend doing anything about it.'

'Why not? A pretty distraction could do you good,' Fraser told him.

Cairn flicked a glance in Gordon's direction.

'Ah, I see. A rival.' Fraser smiled and nodded. 'He wouldn't stand a chance, Cairn, if you were to change your mind and decide to challenge him for Eila's affections.'

'You make it sound like we'd duel at dawn,' Cairn chided him.

'Well, it's all just a bit of fun. My money would be on you, and you know how I hate to be beaten on a bet. Your buckle would definitely outdo his swash.'

Cairn smiled and shook his head.

'That's the third time I've seen you smile this morning. What's wrong with you? How dare you look happy when we've the continuing argument between my father and Hamish to deal with.'

'What's the bone of contention?'

'The film company want us to design suits for them again. Create suits for their leading male actors in a new movie being filmed in the UK,' Fraser explained.

'Why are Sholto and Hamish arguing over that?'

'The request came through late last night from Los Angeles. It was only afternoon there. Anyway, Sholto accepted the deal, but Hamish wanted to cancel or postpone our trip here. He thought we should work on the actors new suit designs in Edinburgh. My father said we could easily work from here, and then they started arguing over it. My cue to leave and come here early. Hopefully they'll have calmed down by the time they arrive.'

'They'll be on their way,' said Cairn.

'Yes, so be ready to talk about the new designs.'

'What type of movie is it this time?'

'An action adventure. Apparently, they want their leading men to look — action–stylish.'

'Action–stylish? That's a new one. But we can do that I'm sure.' Cairn grinned at the thought of this.

‘There you are smiling again, Cairn. I’ll have to become accustomed to this new version of you.’

Cairn forced a serious look.

Fraser laughed. ‘No, there’s a smirk fighting to get out.’

Cairn tried to contain his smile, as they joked with each other.

Shaking themselves dry, they went over to Fraser’s expensive dark car.

Fraser opened the boot and they both got dressed. No joggers and leisure gear for these two men. Only the best in cavalry twill trousers and shirts.

Cairn pulled on a pair of beige trousers and tightened the belt around his honed waistline. He threw a pale blue shirt on and left it unbuttoned, and stepped into a pair of brogues.

Fraser’s trousers and shirt were in neutral tones. Very stylish.

Smoothing his hair back, Fraser got into the car, along with Cairn.

Fraser then drove them away from the shore and up to the house to get ready to welcome Sholto and Hamish.

Eila should’ve jumped straight in the shower, but instead she’d peered out the window of her shop, watching Cairn and Fraser showering, getting dressed and then driving away. If they were trying to put on a distracting performance, they had succeeded in every way. Her heart beat fast just seeing them. And seeing Gordon.

No more distractions! She mentally scolded herself, and moved away from the window. Get cleaned up and ready for work!

CHAPTER TEN

A delivery van pulled up outside Eila's dress shop in the late afternoon.

She frowned. No deliveries were due.

It had been a busy day in the shop, dealing with customers, and lots of sewing. Despite the morning swim, she'd managed to settle into the day and had been determined to sew the dresses and skirts.

The delivery driver waved to her and then he began unloading items.

Eila opened the door and called out to him. 'I wasn't expecting a delivery.'

The driver checked his notes. 'Eila?'

'Yes, but—'

'This is definitely for you.' He smiled and then unloaded a large cardboard box.

Eila stepped aside to let him carry it in. He sat it on the counter.

She stared in surprise and delight when she saw what it was.

'There's more stuff to come,' he chirped, and went out to unload it.

By the time the delivery driver had gone, Eila's shop was restocked with a beautiful selection of fabric. From bolts to pieces large enough to make a dress, plain and patterned, some of her favourite fabrics and others she'd wanted or that were a lovely complement.

Eila stood in her shop, having now closed for the day, and gazed around her. The new sewing machine was unboxed on the counter, and she'd filled the shelves with all the fabric she'd been gifted. For it was a gift — a generous gift from Cairn.

She reread the message from Cairn on her phone and smiled:

By way of thanks for all the information and assistance you've given. Cairn.

She'd replied:

I love the sewing machine, and your fabric selection is perfect. Thank you. Eila.

Tempted by the new sewing machine, she set it up in the shop where she'd planned one day to have a second machine. It was the same make of machine she'd enjoyed using in Cairn's sewing room.

She smiled as it whizzed along the seams of one of the dresses she was making. Oh, yes, she thought. This machine was great.

She was so taken with sewing the dress, and discovering all the handy functions the machine had, that she didn't notice the day fold into twilight.

It was only when someone knocked on the front window and peered in at her that she realised the time.

Gordon smiled in and waved.

She stopped stitching and went over to let him in. She hadn't seen him since the swimming fiasco.

He noticed the well–stocked shelves. 'I heard you'd had a delivery of fabric and other things.'

'No secrets around here, are there?' she said, smiling

'Nope.'

She stepped aside to show him the new sewing machine.

'Very nice. I don't know anything about them, apart from seeing the ones that are set up on quilting bee nights. But that one looks like a beauty. And expensive.'

'Cairn bought it for me,' she came right out and told him, wondering if the gossipmongers knew this snippet of information.

Gordon's smile faded slightly, though he tried to hide his reaction.

She guessed he didn't know. 'It was delivered along with all this new fabric, and these scissors.'

The set of precision scissors gleamed under the lights.

'That was very generous of him.' He tried not to sound as if it grudged him to say this.

She smiled brightly. 'It was. It's by way of payment for the lists and information I've given him.'

'A fair exchange,' he said. 'You deserve it.' He heard the jealousy in his voice and didn't like it. He perked up and changed his attitude. 'You deserve the best, Eila.'

'Thank you, Gordon.'

'I can see you're eager to use your new machine, but I came to ask if you'd like to have dinner at the tea shop.'

She blinked, taken aback by the invitation.

'But I completely understand if you'd prefer to get on with your sewing. I know what I'm like when I get a new mixer. I can't wait to whip up cakes.'

'I'd like to have dinner at the tea shop,' she said, smiling at him. 'I haven't cooked anything, so that would be great.'

Gordon gave no reason for the invitation, no special purpose, no excuse. He'd thought about telling her it was an impromptu tasting night to sample his truffles, but had decided to simply ask her to have dinner with him.

He checked the time. 'I'll be closing the tea shop in about half an hour. Pop along when it suits you.'

'I'll finish up here and them come along,' she said, smiling.

Happy that she'd accepted, he left her, and walked back to the tea shop. His heart felt in danger of falling deeply in love with her. If he was going to risk letting himself hope that she had feelings for him, instead of Cairn, he had to make an impression on her during dinner.

He couldn't buy her an expensive sewing machine like Cairn had. Well, he could. He did well for himself financially, though he wasn't as wealthy as Cairn. But Eila didn't need another one, or fabric by the looks of the well–stocked shelves. He didn't know about fabric either, and Cairn certainly had an advantage over him with that. Cairn understood Eila's business needs better than he did.

Gordon sighed to himself, folded the sandwich board that had advertised the day's specials, including a vanilla cake layered with whipped cream, strawberries and raspberries, and chocolate cupcakes topped with buttercream and chocolate sprinkles.

He intended offering Eila his frittata, but also had other items on the menu if she preferred. His frittata was popular with customers and was a delicious mix of eggs, cream, cherry tomatoes, red peppers, red onion and other tasty vegetables. He planned to serve it up with a crisp green salad and slices of his own fresh baked bread.

Eila brushed her hair, touched up her makeup with a soft rosy lipstick, and wore another one of her favourite tea dresses that always made her feel confident and comfortable. The fabric had a rose and lily of the valley print, and the modern vintage style of the dress suited her perfectly.

Gordon welcomed her in. He'd changed his shirt and wore another clean white shirt. His smile was warm and genuine — it gave her a feeling of coming home and she felt at ease with Gordon and yet...

Under the amber and pink lamps his face was handsome. Gordon had a handsomeness that wore more slowly on the senses but burned deeper and longer. For a moment, she could see herself with this man. Someone she could settle down with.

She shook such thoughts from her mind. What was she thinking? Gordon had been kind enough to offer her dinner at the tea shop. She shouldn't read too much into the gesture, especially as they'd hit it off right away, and had a comfortable friendship since they'd first met.

'I thought we'd sit here.' He showed her over to a table for two tucked out of view of the window. A lantern lit with a candle flickered on the table, and he'd set it up beautifully with napkins and polished cutlery. 'Jock's ceilidh dancing is on tonight and people will be traipsing past the tea shop. I don't want everyone ogling in at us.'

She nodded. 'Our dinner will be hot gossip in the morning without us adding to it tonight.'

The cosy niche suited her and she relaxed while Gordon busied himself preparing their dinner. She'd opted for the frittata, as he'd hoped. He cooked it up expertly while she relaxed.

He spoke to her from the kitchen, and they chatted while he made the tea and cut the bread.

'So you like your new sewing machine?'

'Yes, it made short work of the seams on the tea dress, and it has extra functions for creating a lovely finish on the hem. I love my old machine, and don't mind it's foibles, but it's a treat having something of this calibre to whiz up the dresses.'

'I'm glad you're happy with it,' he called to her. Then he lifted up the pot of tea and brought it through. He set it on a silver trolley beside their table. 'Help yourself to a cuppa while you're waiting. My frittata won't be long. I've found a way to ensure it's never flat. It's all about keeping the eggs fluffy. My frittata is always well–risen.'

She was sure he wasn't boasting, just happy to tell her about his cooking, and she was eager to know his techniques.

Pouring a cup of tea, she relaxed, admired the tea shop, and listened to Gordon bustling around in the kitchen. For the first time since the morning she felt herself unwind.

She sipped her tea. 'I'm taking advantage of you tonight,' she called through to him.

His spatula rattled off his cooking pan.

Realising her faux pas, she quickly explained, 'What I mean is, I'm sitting here and letting you do all the work. You've had a busy day too.'

'I'm happy to cook dinner for you, Eila.'

She heard the contained laughter in his voice and smiled to herself.

While she peeked out at the people going by the window, heading for the ceilidh at the bar restaurant, Gordon finished cooking their meal.

Eila settled down again out of view, tucked cosily in the niche with Gordon as he served up their dinner.

He'd garnished the frittata and salad with fresh parsley and herbs from the garden. 'I grow them myself. Nice and fresh.'

Eila tasted her dinner and nodded enthusiastically. 'This is so delicious.'

'Help yourself to the crusty bread.'

She picked up a thick cut slice. 'You bake your own bread?'

'I enjoy baking — cakes, scones, bread...'

She smiled at him, admiring his handsome face and blue eyes that were lit by the flickering glow of the candle.

They chatted about their day, and she learned more about Gordon's plans to expand his range of chocolates. He gleaned more information on her vintage style tea dresses.

After clearing their plates away, he offered her a choice of cakes.

'I kept a couple of portions of today's special cakes.'

Eila opted for the vanilla cake with whipped cream, strawberries and raspberries, as did Gordon.

'Hang on,' he said as she was about to taste it. He ran through to the kitchen and came back with two glasses of pink champagne and handed one to her. 'It tastes better with this. Enhances the flavour. I like to dip my raspberries into pink champagne before adding them to the cake.'

Eila smiled at him and held up her glass. 'I think this calls for a toast.'

'What shall we drink to?' he asked.

She shrugged, but Gordon had a suggestion. He held up his glass and said, 'To our first night together, as us.'

There was something so touching in his words that her heart squeezed as she tipped her glass against his and took a sip of champagne.

Over champagne, cake and cheerful chatter, they set the worlds to rights.

She couldn't remember the last time she'd had such a warm and happy evening.

The voices of people going past the tea shop window, laughing on their way to the ceilidh, filtered through to them as they finished their meal.

'The ceilidh night must be popular,' Eila commented.

'It is,' he said, and then asked, 'Would you like to go along for a wee while?' This hadn't been his intention. He'd planned to have an evening alone with Eila, but it seemed selfish not to invite her to the ceilidh dancing.

'Yes, I'd like that,' she replied, wondering where she'd get her energy from, but the frittata and cake was kicking in, along with the effects of the champagne.

Gordon cleared the table in a flash and then smiled at her. 'Okay, shall we go?'

Eila eyed him. 'Doesn't Jock frown on men not wearing a kilt?' She'd heard this from chatter at the quilting bee night, and was sure that Judy said that Jock insisted on men wearing one.

Gordon pressed his lips together and nodded. 'He does. So, for you, Eila, I'll whip my trousers off—'

She blinked and sniggered.

'And put my kilt on.' He pointed a scolding finger at her. 'Behave yourself young lady.' Then he ran upstairs to get changed.

'I'm sure you've got the legs for it,' she said, teasing him.

'Yes, and you'll know, because you've seen me without my clothes on, as you put it!'

She liked that their banter was light and cheery.

Eila wandered around and called up to him. 'Permission to have a nosey around your kitchen?'

'Permission granted,' he called down to her.

His kitchen was very tidy, and even after cooking their dinner, it was still clean. Their dishes had been stashed in the dishwasher, and everything was gleaming. 'You're a very tidy worker,' she called up to him, wandering through to where the stairs led down into the front shop.

Unfortunately, it was bad timing, because Gordon was bounding down the stairs in such a hurry that his kilt was swinging up and giving her a glimpse of what he was wearing underneath it. Or rather, what he wasn't wearing.

The gasp and giggle escaped before she could hide her reaction.

'Eila!' he scolded her playfully.

'I didn't see anything,' she lied.

He smiled at her and escorted her out of the tea shop.

The lights shone from the front entrance of the bar restaurant and lively music poured out into the night air.

Eila was glad she'd worn comfy pumps with her dress. She could dance in those.

'Are you into ceilidh dancing?' Gordon asked her as they walked into the function room at the back of the premises.

'I've been to a few. I don't know many dances, but Judy says that Jock is a great instructor.'

Judy and Jock smiled when they saw Eila and Gordon arrive.

'Come away in,' Jock beckoned them. 'The more the merrier.'

The dance floor was busy with people linking arms and whirling around to the lively music.

Soon Eila and Gordon were pulled into the fast–moving reels, laughing and dancing together.

Everything was fine for a little while until four figures arrived to join the ceilidh night. The dancing slowed and people stopped to stare at Sholto, Hamish, Fraser and Cairn, dressed in kilts, standing there.

Judy glared and whispered accusingly to Jock. 'No! You didn't invite them, did you?'

Jock adjusted his sporran. 'Yes, Judy, I did. I had one of the lads run up to their big hoose and give them an invitation.'

'What did you do that for?' Judy hissed at him.

'Because the last time Sholto was here, we were all arguing that he never socialised with any of us. And he accused us of never inviting him to anything. So...' Jock shrugged. 'I never thought they'd accept.'

'Well, they have accepted. What else did you promise on the invitation?' Judy knew Jock only too well.

Jock tightened the buckle on his kilt and looked guilty. 'I said there was a special supper as part of the ceilidh night.'

'There's nothing special about a bowl of broth and a slice of bread, Jock. We haven't cooked anything fancy,' Judy scolded him.

Jock took the scolding and then walked over to welcome their guests.

'Hello there, Sholto. It's been a long time.' He offered his hand and Sholto gave him a firm handshake.

'Thank you for inviting us,' Sholto's voice had a commanding tone, and everyone listened to what he said as the music continued to play. 'It was an unexpected surprise.'

Hamish stepped forward and shook hands with Jock, as did Fraser and Cairn.

Three of them wore kilts made from Sholto's family tartan, and as expected, they were tailored to perfection and teamed with traditional cream shirts and waistcoats. Cairn wore a Black Isle tartan kilt.

Cairn's Ghillie shirt laced up the front and displayed his fine chest and broad shoulders. Fraser and Hamish opted for high collar shirts and ruched ties, while Sholto's classic shirt was worn with a stylish cravat.

Jock took in Sholto's appearance. Although Jock was a few years younger, time had been kind to Sholto. If anything, Sholto looked younger than before, with great posture that made him appear as formidable as his reputation.

All tall in stature, the four of them created an imposing line up even before they started dancing. Because Jock and others knew these men could ceilidh dance with the best of them.

Cairn saw Eila standing with Gordon and nodded over to her. She smiled and nodded back.

Gordon surmised that the two newcomers were Sholto and Hamish. They were as the gossipmongers had described. He'd thought the women at the quilting bee had been exaggerating, but these men were a handsome lot.

Eila saw Cairn whisper to Sholto, and then pale grey eyes targeted her across the dance floor. What a handsome, mature man, she thought to herself. Then she looked at Hamish. He had a shock of burnished amber hair and green eyes, and a strong build. No wonder they set the local women's hearts racing.

As if sensing her thoughts, Gordon squeezed Eila's hand. 'Promise me something,' he said quietly.

'What?'

'When our ceilidh dancing is finished, our night won't be over. Come back with me to the tea shop for a cuppa. Just you and me.' Gordon's blue eyes urged her to say yes.

'I promise,' she said. It was a promise she wanted to keep, for there was a change in the atmosphere of the ceilidh now that Sholto and the others had arrived. A tension in the air, even as the dancing started again.

Jock came hurrying over to Gordon and whispered urgently, 'I've got myself into a pickle.'

'What's wrong?' Gordon asked.

'I sent Sholto and the lads an invitation to the ceilidh night, but...I sort of promised them something special to eat for supper. Judy's not happy with me. We'd only planned to lay on our usual bowl of broth and bread. We've nothing fancy to give them.'

'Leave it to me,' Gordon assured him. 'Fancy is coming right up. I've got cakes in my display cabinets, including a three–layer chocolate gateau with crystallised cherries on top. And I've got plenty of truffles. I'll run next door and be back soon.'

'I'll go with you,' said Jock.

Gordon and Jock scurried away, leaving Eila standing at the side of the dance floor. Minnie waved and was about to pull her into the fast–moving reel, when a smooth voice whispered close to her. 'You look lovely tonight. Would you like to join in the dancing with me?'

She glanced up and saw Cairn gazing at her, holding out his hand.

She found herself taking his hand and letting him lead her on to the floor. 'Thank you for the sewing machine, and the gorgeous fabric,' she told him. 'I've been sewing dresses, and the machine stitches like a dream.'

Cairn smiled, happy that she was pleased with the gifts.

Within moments, they were dancing together, amid the others, smiling and whirling around to the lively music.

But in her mind she kept willing Gordon to hurry up and come back.

CHAPTER ELEVEN

Minnie was dancing at the ceilidh with her friend, Shawn, the big, strapping farmer. He whirled her around the floor, until she insisted she needed a breather.

While Minnie sat the next dance out, Shawn queued at the bar to buy her a lemonade sherry, and she chatted to Eila.

Minnie nudged Eila. 'What do you think of Sholto and his sons?'

'They're very handsome, and Sholto looks impressive,' said Eila.

They weren't short of dance partners. The local ladies were flirting with all of them.

One of the farmer's exuberant daughters flung herself around Fraser during the dancing.

'Sholto can't say they weren't made welcome,' Minnie commented, watching the young woman's father tactfully peeling her off him and escorting her away.

Judy and Pearl hurried over and joined Eila and Minnie. Judy explained that Jock had sent an invitation to Sholto's house.

'Jock didn't expect them to accept the invitation, especially as they've only just arrived,' Judy explained.

'Where did Jock and Gordon run off to?' Pearl asked Judy.

'Jock over promised on the supper menu,' said Judy. 'We've only got broth and bread tonight, nothing fancy. So, Gordon to the rescue. They've run next door to raid the tea shop's cake cabinet and confectionery.'

Pearl leaned close and confided. 'I have some inside gossip from Sholto's house. They've hired local catering staff, and one of the cooks is a friend of mine.'

Eila, Minnie and Judy listened intently.

Pearl continued, 'She says that Sholto and Hamish have been arguing about coming here. They've been given a contract from a film studio to design the suits for the main actors in a new movie. Hamish wanted them to cancel or postpone their trip here, but Sholto dug his heels in and said they could create the new designs here. Hamish wants them to work in Edinburgh. Cairn agrees with Sholto, though he didn't at first.' Pearl flicked a look at Eila. 'Seems Cairn is happy here now. Fraser is undecided, as always. So there's an underlying rumpus going on below the calm surface.'

'Does that mean they might cut their stay short?' Judy asked Pearl.

Pearl shrugged. 'I doubt it'll be as long as they'd originally planned.'

Minnie gasped. 'Don't look now, but Sholto's heading over here. My goodness, that man has a lot of swagger in his kilt.'

'Hamish is coming with him,' Pearl hissed.

Judy pretended they were discussing quilting. 'Have you pieced your new patchwork, Pearl?'

Pearl smiled. 'I have, Judy. I'll bring it along to the quilting bee tomorrow night. Perhaps you can help me decide on the thread colour for the quilting. I usually opt for a light grey so it blends in, but I'm swithering whether to use blue to highlight the design.'

'Good evening, ladies.' Sholto's rich voice cut into their conversation.

'Hello, Sholto.' Minnie sounded miffed, surprised he had the nerve to approach them. The last time she'd seen him, he was arguing with Jock and several other locals, including her, at the last dance he'd given at his house before leaving everyone in the lurch.

Sholto nodded curtly. 'Minnie.' Then he acknowledged Pearl and Judy. His stunning grey eyes swept on to Eila. He waited for a proper introduction.

Minnie introduced them. 'Eila, this is Sholto and Hamish.'

Sholto looked at Eila. 'I've heard about you from Cairn. Thank you for your input regarding fabric suppliers.'

'You're welcome.' Eila smiled tightly, feeling Sholto's gaze assessing her.

Hamish extended his hand to Eila. 'Delighted to meet you.'

Up close Hamish was classically handsome, with gorgeous green eyes and a sexy smile. He suited wearing a kilt, she thought. It enhanced his tall, strong but fit build.

A friend of Shawn elbowed his way through the bar crowd to where Shawn was standing at the front ordering Minnie's lemonade sherry.

'Would you like a cherry with that?' the bartender asked, familiar with Minnie's taste.

'Yes, thanks,' Shawn confirmed.

'Shawn!' his friend hissed to him. 'Shawn!'

Shawn looked round at him.

The man thumbed over his shoulder. 'Sholto and Hamish are hanging around your Minnie. You'd better get over there.'

Shawn reacted immediately, striding through to the function room and approaching Minnie.

'Here's your drink, Minnie,' Shawn said, cutting between Sholto and Hamish. Normally, Shawn was used to being the tallest and broadest shouldered man, but standing beside Sholto and Hamish he felt his stature diminished. Without hesitation, he whisked Minnie away from temptation. Not that he didn't trust her, but he'd heard a few local men complain about their wives and girlfriends being distracted by Sholto, his sons and Cairn.

Hamish smiled at Eila and held out his hand. 'Are you up for a reel?'

'Eh, yes.' Eila accepted Hamish's offer and within moments they were dancing, holding hands and whirling around the dance floor.

Every now and again, she glanced through to the bar, and saw Gordon and Jock hurrying in loaded with cake boxes.

Gordon carried the supper items behind the bar into the kitchen. He tried to ignore that his heart felt skewered having seen Hamish dancing happily with Eila. Once again, he'd missed his chance to impress her, but he needed to help Jock.

'I'm really grateful, Gordon,' Jock said, putting the cakes down in the kitchen.

Gordon tapped a large tub of soup. 'There are around six portions of cock–a–leekie soup in there.' He'd served it that day at the tea shop, and reserved some for his dinner date with Eila. She hadn't eaten soup for her dinner, but he'd planned to offer her his special cock–a–leekie as a late night treat after the ceilidh. However, Jock was in a bind, so he'd given it to him.

'This will allow you to offer Sholto the choice of broth or cock–a–leekie, so keep it for them,' Gordon advised.

'That's a great idea. I'll do that,' said Jock. 'And thank you for the impressive cakes and chocolate truffles.'

Judy came hurrying through to the kitchen, eager to see what they'd foraged. 'The chocolate gateau looks magnificent. I've settled Sholto and the others at a table and I'm about to offer them the menu.' She wrote down the other items on offer. 'Right, I'll pop out and see what they fancy.'

'No, Judy,' said Jock. 'I'll go and face them myself.'

Judy nodded. 'Great, I'll start organising the suppers for everyone.'

Two members of staff were set to help her. Plates rattled, water boiled for the tea, and the broth and cock–a–leekie soup were bubbling away on standby.

Jock tucked a notepad and pencil in his sporran and ventured out into the bar restaurant.

Judy sighed and shook her head. 'I hope this hasn't ruined your dinner date with Eila.'

Gordon smiled. 'No, I'm only too glad to help you out of a pickle. Eila has promised to come back with me to the tea shop after the ceilidh. And I'm sure I'll get a dance with her after the suppers are served.'

Judy eyed the chocolate gateau. 'If they want the gateau, I'd rather you cut it expertly.'

Gordon put on a clean apron. He washed and dried his hands, then set up a large, crusty loaf he'd brought that hadn't even been cut into. It was fresh baked that day.

Judy didn't say anything as Gordon commandeered part of the kitchen. He cut the bread, as if anticipating an order for it.

'We've got plenty of crusty bread ready for serving,' Judy told him.

'This is for something else. Jock and I added doorsteps to the menu for Sholto. I'm betting at least one of them will want one.'

Judy mentally prepared to give Jock a firm telling off later, but she was grateful that Gordon was mucking in to make their night a success in front of Sholto.

Gordon set up the cheese board, and cut thin slices of his traditional Scottish Cheddar cheese. He'd brought a jar of his raspberry chutney and opened it ready.

Checking the fridge, he saw they had prepared fresh green salad and tomatoes, but he'd brought a couple of yellow tomatoes with him for garnishing.

Jock came hurrying back in, beaming with delight. 'Two broths and two cock–a–leekies,' he read off from his notes. 'Sholto and Hamish fancy the leekie.'

Gordon smiled to himself, glad that he'd offered it.

Judy jumped into action, ladling out the broth while Gordon scooped two generous portions of the leekie into bowls.

'I'll serve it up myself,' said Jock, taking charge of the trays of soup and the basket brimming with bread. And off he went, disappearing out of the kitchen.

'Round one down,' said Gordon. 'Let's see if they're temped by the doorsteps.' He raided the fridge for other garnishes, including red onion and tomatoes.

'Four doorsteps with all the works,' Jock announced, bounding in, ticking the order on his notes.

Gordon buttered the thick slices of loaf, spread them with the raspberry chutney and then layered them with the cheese, red onion, tomatoes, and salad ingredients. He added ground black pepper, sea salt and served them up on plates with a garnish flourish.

'You've done us proud, Gordon.' Jock smiled at him and carried the doorsteps through to the bar restaurant.

Gordon used up everything he'd brought, giving others an extended supper menu where possible.

Jock came in rubbing his hands together. 'Three chocolate gateau and one raspberry and cream meringue.'

Judy tried to guess the odd one out. 'Cairn?'

Jock shook his head, while Gordon cut three slices of gateau. The cherries were glazed on the top of each slice. He also made sure the raspberry cream meringue had a chocolate truffle on the plate.

'Fraser?' said Judy.

'Nah, it's Hamish,' Jock told her.

After serving up their cakes, Jock came into the kitchen and sighed heavily. 'We did it. Sholto said he was impressed.'

Gordon felt the effort had been worth it.

'It's unlikely that Sholto will set foot in here again,' said Jock, 'but he's got a different impression of us now.'

Gordon cut the rest of the cake up for other customers, while Jock and Judy confided beside the sink.

'Agreed,' said Judy. 'Tell Sholto their supper is on the house. They were invited as our guests tonight.'

Jock smiled with glee and hurried through to tell them.

Moments later, Jock ran back in. 'Gordon, would you mind coming through to talk to Sholto for a minute.'

Gordon hesitated.

Jock shrugged. 'I blabbed that you were responsible for the excellent cooking. Credit where credit's due.'

Gordon hadn't wanted any credit. He just wanted to help out.

'Come on,' Jock beckoned him. 'Just show your face and then away and dance with Eila.'

Gordon took his apron off, hung it up, glanced at Judy as she tried not to smile, and went through to the bar restaurant.

'Here's the man responsible for your tasty supper,' Jock announced. 'This is Gordon.'

Sholto stood up and shook hands with him. 'You're an excellent cook. One of the hardest things in cuisine is to make basic fayre outstanding. You did that tonight with soup, a sandwich and cake.'

'It was perfect for an evening like this,' Cairn was generous to admit.

'I'm glad you all liked it.' Gordon smiled.

'Jock tells me you own the tea shop,' said Sholto.

'I do.'

Sholto picked up one of the extra truffles that Jock had added to their plates. 'He says you have your own range of confectionery.'

'Yes, it's a recent addition to my business,' Gordon told Sholto.

'I'll be ordering some boxes of these from you,' said Sholto.

Gordon smiled and nodded.

'And I'll be in for afternoon tea,' Fraser added.

'I'll look forward to seeing you,' said Gordon.

With the pleasantries concluded, Gordon left them and went to find Eila. She was sitting chatting to Minnie, Shawn and Pearl.

Eila brightened when she saw Gordon approach.

'Shall we get back to our dancing?' Gordon asked her.

'Yes,' she said, taking his hand and letting him lead her into one of the reels.

At the bar, Jock made jugs of his special cocktail that was enjoyed by the revellers. Glasses were filled with the potent concoction, sending the merriment into the danger zone. Danger only of it being the best ceilidh night in a long time.

Jock joined in the dancing. He'd thought that Sholto's participation would put a slight dampener on the evening, but it didn't at all.

Gordon was amazed to find himself linking arms and whirling around the floor with Cairn, laughing with him, and then jigging with Sholto during the men's only routine.

While the men danced, the ladies stood around the edge of the dance floor clapping and cheering them on.

Eila stood beside Minnie.

'I never thought I'd see Sholto, Hamish, Fraser and Cairn dancing with Jock, Gordon and Shawn.' Minnie clapped but looked amazed.

Eila nodded, and looking at the incredulous but happy expression on Gordon's face, he hadn't expected this either.

It was one of those evenings, Eila thought, letting the dancing and music waft around her, where everything had worked out well for all those involved. A night to remember. Dancing was a great leveller, she concluded, smiling at Gordon whirling around the floor with Sholto and Jock.

As the ladies joined in the dancing again, Eila found herself dancing with Cairn, Hamish, Fraser and Sholto as well as Gordon and Jock. The atmosphere was cheerful and she knew she'd remember this as one of the top ceilidh nights she'd ever enjoyed.

As the evening finally finished and people headed home, Gordon stood outside and wondered if Eila would keep her promise. He wouldn't hold her to it, he thought, as the dancing had continued until late, and their plans had gone awry from the start.

But Eila intended keeping her promise, and smiled at Gordon, waiting for him to invite her into the tea shop.

Gordon's expectations soared. 'It's late, but would you like to come in for a cup of tea before going home?'

'Yes. A cup of tea would be lovely.' She'd been plied with Jock's cocktails and although she'd gone easy on them, she welcomed a refreshing cup of tea to settle her for the night.

Gordon led her inside the tea shop. Lights were on and there was mild chaos where Jock had helped him ransack the contents of the cake display cabinets.

She followed him through to the kitchen and he started to make the tea.

'Would you like anything to go with your tea?' he offered.

'Tea would be fine.' She'd eaten enough chocolate truffles and didn't feel like eating anything sweet or substantial.

'How about some hot buttered toast?'

This sounded tasty. 'If you're having some, then yes.'

Gordon fired up the grill and within minutes the bread was toasting nicely.

'Do you usually attend Jock's ceilidh nights?' she asked him.

'Sometimes, but usually if I've been working all day from the early morning, I like to relax upstairs and watch one of my favourite films or TV shows. I'm following a series at the moment and haven't caught up on the latest episodes.'

He mentioned the show and she recognised it. 'I've love spy thrillers like that. I'd been following it, then I became so busy with moving here. What part are you up to?'

'Jay is suspicious of his brother–in–law and now he doesn't trust his wife. He's found out that there's a British secret agent following him, spying on him.'

'What a cliffhanger! I remember watching that episode. What happened?'

'I don't know. I haven't had time to watch the next episode.'

Eila sighed and nodded. 'I must make time to relax and watch it.'

Gordon buttered their toast. 'Would you like to pop up and watch half an hour of it while we have our tea and toast?'

She blinked. She really wanted to, but it was late and...

'Just have tea and toast and watch a bit of telly,' he assured her. 'Nothing more.'

'Okay.'

Gordon led the way upstairs. His flat was comfortably furnished and tidy. The decor was light and the lighting cosy. He had a wonderful view of the sea from his living room window.

They sat down on the sofa and put their tea on the coffee table.

'The quilting bee ladies made this quilt for me, and the quilted cushions,' he told her. 'If you see anything quilted, they made it for me.'

'It looks lovely,' she said, admiring the living room and the quilted items. A patchwork quilt was folded on the arm of the sofa, and some of the cushion covers matched it.

Gordon flicked the television on, set up the next episode of the series, and they settled down to watch it while having their tea and toast.

Eila couldn't remember feeling so relaxed and at home, and yet...she was attracted to Gordon...

The cliffhanger was revealed at the start of the episode, and their plan to watch half an hour extended into the full episode and the following one.

Midway through the second episode, Eila felt herself drifting off...

The next thing she knew, the dawn was breaking over the sea and Gordon's alarm was going off in his sporran. He blinked awake, jarred by the alarm on his phone, and fumbled to flick it off.

They stared at each other as the realisation kicked in — they'd fallen asleep together on the sofa. She'd woken up with her head resting on his shoulder and the quilt was shared between them.

Eila was sure that nothing intimate had happened between them, and thought the situation was quite funny.

'We must've fallen asleep,' Gordon gasped. He checked the time. 'It's my early morning alarm.'

When he said early morning he wasn't kidding. She glanced out the window. 'The dawn is barely up.'

He smiled and then they both started laughing.

'I'd better get back to my shop,' she said, gathering herself.

'Yes, of course. I hope you don't think I was trying to take advantage of you.'

'No, not at all. We were both exhausted from all that dancing.'

'And the fiasco with the morning swim.'

'That too,' she agreed, wondering if he'd go swimming that morning. She was sure she wouldn't be venturing into the sea today.

Eila hurried downstairs and Gordon opened the tea shop door.

She felt the need to peer out. 'I'm checking that the coast is clear. If Minnie or anyone sees me leaving...well...'

'More gossip.'

'Exactly.'

There was no one around so she smiled and hurried away.

'I'll call you later, Eila. Thanks for a great night.'

Eila looked round to wave and that's when she saw Euan striding along. The look on his face said it all. She smiled and nodded pleasantly at Euan and then scurried into her shop and locked the door.

She sighed heavily, knowing her unintentional sleepover at the tea shop would be the topic of the morning. And she hadn't so much as kissed Gordon! She'd wanted to. She remembered wondering if he'd kiss her, then she must've fallen asleep.

Euan couldn't keep the gossip to himself.

'Eila was scrambling out of Gordon's tea shop at this early hour?' Minnie exclaimed. Then she smiled. 'I'm happy for them. They make a lovely couple.'

Euan had been at the ceilidh and had seen everything that had gone on that night.

'Eila and Gordon danced well together,' Euan observed. 'But she danced with Cairn too. I think Cairn has a strong fancy for her.'

'Eila danced with most of the men, and so did I.'

Euan nodded. 'But there was an attraction between Eila and Cairn, definitely stronger on his part. I believe that under different circumstances, Cairn would make a move on her for himself.'

'Cairn belongs to another world. One of them would have to give up everything for the other. I don't think they could merge easily. Eila would have to move to Edinburgh, and I know she's from Glasgow, so maybe the city would suit her. But she's fitted so well into the local community, and Gordon is a lovely man.'

'I hope Gordon makes some bold moves and doesn't let Cairn sweep Eila away with him.'

Minnie nodded thoughtfully.

CHAPTER TWELVE

Oooh! Eila!

Eila read the message on her phone from Minnie and smiled. She replied:

Nothing happened. We watched the telly and fell asleep.

Did he kiss you?

Nope.

I'll hear all about it at the quilting bee tonight.

I suppose everyone will know by then.

Sorry, Eila!

Eila smiled again and put her phone aside. She continued using her new sewing machine to stitch one of the tea dresses.

She gazed out the dress shop window at the sea. There was no sign of Gordon, but she thought he would be busy in his tea shop baking cakes and scones.

But as she worked at her sewing machine, she saw Gordon heading down to the shore. He was dressed in his swimming trunks and carried his rolled up towel.

She watched him put the towel down on the sand, walk towards the calm water that this morning reflected the light from the pale sunshine. It looked so calm and inviting, and she was sorely tempted to throw her skirt and top off and run and join him, but she didn't. They both needed time to themselves, some breathing room to assess how they felt about each other.

And yet...she knew how she felt about Gordon. In a way, she always had, from those first mornings watching his daily dips in the sea — the handsome man, on his own, swimming in the dawn light no matter the weather. She had admired him then and she admired him now.

Of course, she found Cairn attractive. Few women wouldn't. Cairn was extraordinary, but last night as she danced with him, she realised something. She admired his handsomeness, but her heart didn't squeeze and ache to be with him. That feeling was kept exclusively for Gordon.

She gazed out at him swimming into the distance. What was he thinking, she wondered. Then a stab of panic went through her.

Gordon hadn't kissed her. Minnie's question was reasonable, especially under the circumstances of what was essentially a date night with Gordon.

But she was sure that Gordon liked her, more than liked her. She was sure of his feelings for her. Wasn't she?

The quilting bee night was busy. The function room at the back of the tea shop was buzzing with activity and chatter.

As Eila expected, the gossip highlights included Sholto, Hamish, Fraser and Cairn turning up at the ceilidh. And the cherry on the top of the gossip was her cosy sleepover with Gordon.

Eila attempted to divert the conversation towards the topic of the television series, rather than reveal that she'd snuggled under one of their quilts on the sofa with Gordon.

'I haven't caught up on that episode of the spy thriller series,' said Pearl. 'Did Jay fly to London with the British secret agent?'

Judy cut–in and cupped her hands over her ears. 'Don't tell me what happens. I'm one episode behind that. No spoilers please.'

Eila zipped her lips, and the conversation focussed on her sleepover with Gordon.

'It sounds like you had a cosy night with our Gordon,' Minnie began. 'Did he toast your crumpet for you?'

The women giggled, teasing Eila.

'Minnie!' Eila gasped, trying not to laugh as Gordon sauntered by with a cake stand brimming with chocolate and strawberry cupcakes and fruit scones filled with cream and bramble jam.

'My ears are burning,' Gordon commented as he put the cake stand on a table.

The women laughed.

'Oh, come on,' Minnie said to him, helping herself to a strawberry cupcake that was swirled with buttercream. 'The pair of you were kippered after dancing your socks off.'

Gordon glanced at Eila for back–up, but she hid behind a cream and bramble jam scone, trying not to smile. Minnie had summed up their evening. Everyone knew what had happened.

'In my defence,' Gordon announced, 'I'd been swimming with sharks in the morning and dancing my kilt off at night.'

'As long as that's all you had off,' Minnie said, laughing.

'Minnie!' Gordon scolded her. 'Behave yourself.'

Eila burst out laughing. 'The look on Gordon's face when he woke up because his phone alarm was ringing and jumping about in his sporran was priceless.'

'I'm glad you're amused, young lady,' Gordon told her, pretending to sound peeved.

'I did like the quilt you'd made for Gordon,' said Eila. 'The patchwork on his sofa. I'm still keen to learn how to sew quilts like that.'

'You'll learn these skills from us at the bee,' Minnie assured her. 'Everyone shares their knowledge so that the skills are passed on to new quilters.'

Eila remembered she'd brought a selection of embroidery thread with her. She dug the skeins of it out of her sewing bag. 'I brought these new colours to share around.'

Several hands were eager to take one, admire the embroidery thread and pass it around.

'Lovely thread,' Pearl enthused. 'I bought a few in the blue tones and I'm planning on embroidering a seahorse. I have a nice pattern for one.'

Pearl and Judy had both been in to Eila's shop and purchased embroidery thread, so they passed the skeins on to other members.

'Has Fraser been in for his afternoon tea?' Judy asked. She'd heard that he planned to do this.

'He was in this afternoon,' Gordon confirmed, taking quite a few of the ladies by surprise. He checked the time. 'In fact, Fraser's due here in a few minutes.'

The women were taken aback. They glanced at Eila but she knew nothing about it. But to be fair, she hadn't had time to speak to Gordon all day, and hadn't seen him until the quilting bee.

Minnie frowned. 'Fraser? He's coming here tonight?'

Even Pearl knew nothing about this.

As if on cue, Fraser walked into the tea shop, elegantly dressed in a dark grey suit, shirt and tie. Cairn was with him.

Gordon didn't expect Fraser to turn up with Cairn. He didn't think that Cairn was interested in his chocolate making techniques, something that Fraser had expressed an interest in during the afternoon.

'What's Cairn doing here?' Eila said to Gordon. 'And what's Fraser doing here for that matter?'

Gordon summarised the details. 'When Fraser was in for afternoon tea, he expressed an interest in my truffles and chocolates. He'd trained in that type of work, and asked if he could view me making them. I was planning on making some while the quilting bee was on, so I invited him along. But I don't know why Cairn is with him.'

Fraser saw Gordon and headed through to the function room, followed by Cairn.

Fraser shook hands with Gordon. 'Thanks for inviting me.'

'I'm about to go through in a few minutes,' said Gordon. 'I'm just settling the ladies with their tea and supper.'

Fraser and Cairn smiled at the ladies, sending their hearts fluttering and curiosity soaring.

Gordon continued to fuss with the teas and serving the cakes.

Fraser took an interest in the dress that Eila had been hemming. She'd sewn only a few stitches as she'd been too busy chatting and gossiping.

'Is that one of your own designs, Eila?' Fraser leaned down to study the dress, feeling the fabric. 'Nice cotton.'

Eila smiled up at him. 'Thank you, Fraser.'

Those grey eyes of his looked at her. 'I trust you'll bring samples of your work with you when you come up to the house for dinner.'

'Eh, yes, I will,' she replied, not having secured a date for the dinner.

Cairn spoke up. 'Sholto would like to know if you could join us tomorrow evening?'

Eila didn't have any plans, and so she accepted the invitation. 'Yes, that would be fine.'

'I'll pick you up again, as before,' Cairn said, smiling at her.

It was the way Cairn smiled that set Gordon on edge, but he sucked up the urge to comment. He knew she was going back to have dinner with them when Sholto arrived. Things were different now and he felt close to Eila, but that didn't stop him from feeling slightly worried that she'd once again be in the company of Cairn.

'Would you like to come through to the kitchen?' Gordon said to Fraser, ushering him away from Eila.

Cairn smiled at Eila. 'See you tomorrow night. And I love that dress too.'

And off they went, both going with Gordon into the kitchen.

'Well,' Minnie said, 'that was a bit of a surprise.' She looked at Eila.

Eila shrugged. 'I guess I'm having another trip to the house. Anyone planning on skulking around in the bushes?'

Minnie shook her head, as did Judy and Pearl.

The majority of the bee members knew what had gone on, and smiled at them.

'Gordon seemed a bit miffed that you're having dinner with them tomorrow night,' Judy commented.

Eila nodded. 'He did, but it's just a business dinner.'

'I'm eager to know what Fraser is up to in the kitchen,' said Pearl with a mischievous look.

Minnie put her quilting down and grinned. 'Shall we?'

Several of the ladies nodded and scurried through to take a peek into the kitchen.

Unfortunately, Cairn was on his way out, and they almost clashed in the kitchen doorway.

Cairn smirked and shook his head at them.

None of the women uttered a word, and simply turned around and went back to the function room to continue their quilting, sewing and knitting.

Cairn sat at a small table at the window of the tea shop. He had a view into the function room. Moments later, Gordon served up tea and cake to him, then hurried back into the kitchen.

Eila tried to concentrate on her sewing and chatting to the women, but every now and then she couldn't help being drawn to Cairn. He'd taken his jacket off and sat with his shirt, tie and waistcoat on, relaxing with one arm draped casually over the back of the chair, drinking his tea, deep in thought.

Cairn took a call and then put his phone away.

The chatter swirled around Eila. She joined in with the chat, but glanced again at Cairn. Perhaps it was the vintage setting of the tea shop and his classic clothes, but he looked like he belonged on a magazine cover, a handsome and timeless picture.

For a second he glanced at her and they looked at each other for a moment longer than either of them should. Maybe she was mistaken, but she sensed he was a bit sad, as if thinking of what might have been between them, as was she. Neither of them belonged in the other's world. One would have to forgo everything. In that moment she sensed they both were thinking this.

The look Cairn finally gave her was burned into her heart forever. A look of what might have been but never was or would be. And then he looked away and gazed out at the view of the sea.

Her heart ached, and then she folded the moment over, like the page of a fiction book that she would remember, but that was never going to be part of her real world.

One of the sewing bee ladies came hurrying over to Eila, Minnie and the others from the front of the tea shop. 'I had a peek in the kitchen and saw Gordon showing Fraser how to make chocolates.'

'Fraser's mother owns a cookery school, and had hoped that Fraser would become a chocolatier or patisserie chef. Fraser had a knack for baking and trained to quite a high level as a chef,' said Pearl.

'But he decided to work in tailoring with his father,' Minnie added.

'Maybe Fraser still has an interest in chocolatier work,' said Eila.

They were so deep in conversation that they didn't notice Cairn approach.

'Yes, Fraser was interested in Gordon's technique for shining his bonbons,' Cairn told them. 'Gordon said he was making chocolate bonbons this evening with a mirror glaze and invited Fraser to pop along.'

'Is Fraser still thinking of becoming a chocolatier?' Minnie asked Cairn.

'No, but he enjoys baking as a hobby,' said Cairn.

'Cairn!' Fraser beckoned to him. 'Come and take a photo of Gordon and me making chocolates.'

Cairn smiled at the ladies and then walked away to the kitchen.

Fraser stood beside Gordon with the chocolates, and Cairn snapped a few pictures with his phone.

Cairn then left Fraser with Gordon and headed out of the tea shop. He cast a look into the quilting bee hub and saw Eila engrossed in her sewing amid the other ladies. She didn't see him leave and drive away.

At the end of the evening the bee members filtered out of the tea shop. Fraser and Gordon emerged from the kitchen. Gordon had served customers in the tea shop while Fraser made chocolates in the kitchen. They emerged together, smiling, and Fraser was delighted with the box of chocolates he'd made.

'Thank you again, Gordon,' Fraser said, heading out with his chocolates. 'I thoroughly enjoyed myself.' He held the box up and nodded to Eila. 'See you at dinner tomorrow, though I doubt there will be any of these chocolates left once I take them to show my father and Hamish.'

Eila and Gordon waved Fraser off, and now that they were left alone in the tea shop, Gordon took a moment to talk to her.

'Did you have an enjoyable evening?' he asked her.

'Yes, I even got some sewing done.' She smiled at him.

They both paused.

'Well, I'm going to try and get an earlier night tonight,' she said. 'I plan to make an early start on my sewing in the morning.'

'I'll see you sometime tomorrow,' he said hopefully. 'But if I don't see you before you have dinner with Sholto, I hope you have a nice time. And you're welcome to pop in afterwards to have tea with me. I'll be working late.'

She nodded, feeling that they'd sort of arranged another date.

Gordon waved Eila off, trying not to show that he was concerned about her having dinner with Cairn again.

Eila's day started as early as she'd intended after a good night's sleep. The entire day was a blur of activity — sewing, packing orders and dealing with customers. Before she knew it, she had to hurry to get ready for dinner. Cairn was due to pick her up soon.

She tidied her hair and wore a really classy tailored dress and court shoes. No wrap around dress tonight. This was tailored to fit and was two shades of grey. She'd made it herself and thought it was appropriate for her dinner with Sholto.

A car pulled up outside the shop, and she picked up her bag, shrugged on one of the tailored jackets she'd made, and hurried out.

But it wasn't Cairn's car. The car belonged to Hamish.

Eila went over and got in the passenger seat.

'Cairn's gone to Edinburgh on business,' said Hamish, driving off.

'Oh, so Cairn won't be having dinner with us?' She hoped he hadn't heard the slight disappointment in her voice.

'No, but my father, Fraser and I are looking forward to discussing your designs.' Hamish smiled and drove them past the tea shop.

Eila glanced out the window and saw Gordon standing at the door. He smiled and nodded to her, and she smiled back at him.

Hamish spoke about their business during the short drive to the house.

As before, it was lit up and the front door was open in welcome.

She expected to be invited into the dining room, but instead, Hamish led her straight through to the sewing room.

The house felt different this evening. With Sholto there driving everything, it had become a place of business not home. Progress was expected, and her visit there was just another item on the agenda.

'My father and Fraser are in here,' said Hamish. 'We've been thrown a curve ball, but we've decided to make the catch and play the game.'

Eila wasn't sure what Hamish meant, but she soon realised that the sense of urgency she felt emanating from the sewing room was due to the so–called curve ball.

'Eila!' Sholto said in welcoming, pleased to see her. 'Come in.' He glanced at Hamish. 'Did you tell Eila what's happened?'

'No, I thought we'd explain when she got here,' Hamish replied.

'What's happened?' she asked. 'If you're busy and have to cancel dinner, it's fine. I'll go home.'

'No, we'll be having dinner,' Sholto assured her, 'but we have to deal with this first. We're all throwing in our ideas, so let's have your opinion, a fresh, young eye, a woman's view, a dressmaker's knowledge.'

This all sounded like a tall order, and she felt her heart race in anticipation of their expectations of her.

Before she could ask what they wanted to know, Sholto said to her, 'First class tailoring on that dress and jacket you're wearing. I assume you made it yourself to your own design.'

'I did, thank you.'

Sholto then continued, 'You know about the film company deal. Making suits for the lead actors.' There were pictures of the actors on Sholto's desk. She recognised them. They were popular stars.

'Yes,' she said, sensing that long babbling answers weren't required in Sholto's world.

'This evening they contacted us and said that they need the designs for the suits earlier than scheduled. They're starting filming sooner than planned. So they've asked us to provide the designs as soon as we have them available.'

Fraser handed Eila samples of colours and fabrics. 'These were sent to us from the set designers.'

Eila studied the various colours and fabric textures. 'These look like wallpaper and paint colour charts.'

'Basically, they are,' said Fraser.

'They surely don't want your suits to match the wallpaper,' Eila scoffed.

'No,' said Sholto, 'but they're creating a certain look for specific scenes. An atmosphere. You know the sort of scene in films where everything blends in tones of one or two hues.'

Eila nodded. 'Yes, scenes where the lighting, the costumes and the background have a colour theme.'

Sholto sighed, 'We can create suits that will blend with the neutral tones of the sets, but the one that's a challenge is the set designer's burgundy theme. Burgundy is difficult for the type of suits we were planning.'

Eila looked around the sewing room. She wandered over to one of the shelves that was filled with suiting fabric. 'Cairn showed me the fabrics you had. I remember there was one...' She pulled out a bolt of fabric and put it down on a table. Under the lights she pointed to the fine burgundy stripe within the mid grey subtle check. 'It reminded me of a fabric I used once for a skirt suit.'

'Yes, the burgundy is there, yet blends with the grey,' said Sholto, eyeing the fabric.

Eila hurried over to a cupboard where Cairn had shown her a beautiful selection of silk ties of various colours, from neutrals to rich jewel tones, including burgundy. There were two burgundy ties. She lifted them off the tie rack and put them down on the suit fabric.

'I wouldn't even go with a burgundy shirt,' she said. 'I'd keep the shirt white or a light neutral, and use the tie to add the burgundy colour.'

Sholto nodded and smiled. 'I like that idea.'

Hamish agreed. 'I think we can go with that.'

Fraser nodded and showed her another colour theme the set designer had sent them. 'This has a subtle blue theme. We've been looking at the fabric colour combinations you sent in the blue tones.'

For the next hour all thoughts of dinner were cast aside in favour of hammering out the fabrics, colour combinations, textures and themes to blend with the film sets.

Hamish read from one of the film company notes. 'The actors must become a part of the setting, without their suits distracting from the scene, but still maintain a classy stylishness.'

Eila looked around at all the beautiful fabrics in the room. 'You've surely got enough here to select from.'

'Nearly,' said Sholto. 'But we've ordered some of those new blues and grey from the suppliers you listed. The fabric will be delivered to Edinburgh.'

Eila blinked. 'Edinburgh?'

'Yes,' Sholto explained. 'We're going to have to cut short our visit here, postpone it until later when the film deal is finished. That's why I sent Cairn ahead of us. He's handling all aspects of the financial deal. No one better than Cairn. I've never known him beaten on a deal yet. He's sharp and cool headed.'

'When do you think you'll leave for Edinburgh?' Eila asked Sholto.

'A few days. But we'll be back for a proper and longer stay as planned, maybe later in the year,' Sholto told her.

'Will we have dinner now?' Hamish said to Sholto. 'I'm sure we could all do with something to eat.'

Sholto nodded and everyone was ushered through to the dining room.

The meal was delicious, and Eila opted for the pasta and a glass of wine. The discussions over dinner were all business related. Pleasant, but business.

They didn't linger long after dinner, and Hamish drove Eila home while Sholto and Fraser went back to work on the designs in the sewing room.

As Hamish dropped her off outside her dress shop, she smiled and waved to him, wondering if she'd see him again. Perhaps she would, but not for a long time. But it wasn't really Hamish she was thinking about, it was Cairn. He'd gone back home to Edinburgh. She thought about how she felt for a moment as a cold breeze blew in from the sea, causing her to shiver, and feel a bit sad. As if she'd lost something she'd never really had.

'Eila!' Gordon shouted to her from the front of the tea shop. He waved and beckoned to her.

Smiling, she hurried over and was glad to feel the warmth of the tea shop, and Gordon's welcome, as she stepped inside.

'You look pale. Everything okay?' he asked her.

'Cairn's gone back to Edinburgh, and Sholto, Hamish and Fraser are leaving here soon.'

Gordon frowned. 'They're all going home to Edinburgh? So soon?'

She explained the reasons.

'I'll make us tea. Would you like something to eat?'

She wasn't sure. The events of the night had thrown her feelings into turmoil. Dinner was fine, but she'd picked at her food, so busy talking about the fabrics and suit designs. Her plates were cleared while still barely touched.

She opened her bag and brought out a white envelope. 'Sholto insisted in giving me this for helping them. He said I should invest it in my business or keep it for a rainy day.'

Gordon peeked at the amount on the cheque. His brows raised and he nodded firmly. 'Generous.'

Eila put the envelope back in her bag. 'I think I will keep it for a rainy day.'

'You should.'

Eila watched Gordon make the tea and was glad to be there with him. She started to feel better.

'Would you mind making toast, like we had before?'

Gordon smiled and fired up the grill. 'Hot buttered toast coming right up.'

Snuggled under the quilt on the sofa, drinking tea and eating toast, they watched the next episode of the television series.

Before she started to fall asleep, Eila put her jacket on and headed back to her shop.

'See you tomorrow, Eila,' Gordon called to her and waved.

She waved back at him and smiled. Yes, she thought, she would see Gordon tomorrow. He hadn't kissed her yet, but she felt he wanted to, and they were both waiting on the right moment.

The next few days were busy, bright and cheerful.

Eila's dress shop thrived, and she enjoyed popping into the tea shop to have cosy chats and tea with Gordon. In the evenings she'd needed to work on sewing the dresses and skirts, and cutting fabric bundles that were popular with customers, including the quilting bee members.

Gordon was busy working on his confectionery range, and creating new season recipes for the tea shop. He'd planned a lovely autumn selection of cakes and hearty savoury flans. The menu items included chestnuts, walnuts, sweet potato soup, spiced apple cakes and tea bread.

It was early evening when Sholto stood outside the bar restaurant to talk to Jock. They were alone. A light breeze blew along the coast, and the vast grey sky arched across the sea.

Sholto was leaving to go home to Edinburgh, but he wanted to have a word with Jock before he drove off.

'I know we've had our differences in the past, Jock, but I'm hoping that's behind us now.'

'It is, Sholto.' Jock thought about the recent ceilidh night, and agreed that the air had been cleared that evening, dancing, having fun and not expecting too much from each other.

'We're all going home to Edinburgh, but I wanted to assure you that we'll back. I don't know when. But when we do, I don't want things to rattle back down to the bad feelings of before. I'm not leaving folks in the lurch, like the last time.'

'You'd every right to pack your bags after the party and go back to Edinburgh,' Jock told him.

Sholto nodded. 'But I know that people felt miffed, slighted. I don't want to leave that feeling this time. We're coming back. It could be a while. Our visit is postponed, not completely cancelled. We'd felt part of the community recently, and we'd like to keep it that way.'

'So would we,' Sholto assured him.

Sholto took a white envelope from the jacket pocket of his expensive suit. 'I'm not sure when your next fete is, but you're one of the main organisers.'

'I am,' Jock confirmed.

'We'd like to contribute to the fund. This should help with the costs of hiring the stalls or for whatever you need it for.' Sholto handed the envelope containing a substantial cheque to Jock. He pointed at it. 'That includes the hire of a stall for us. We're taking part the next time we're here if one is available during a fete.'

Jock smiled. It was clear they no longer wanted to be the outsiders. The cheque would provide great benefit to all those involved. 'Thank you, and I'll explain your thoughts to everyone. I'm sure they'll appreciate this as much as I do.'

Sholto held out his hand. It was time to go. 'All the best to you, Jock.'

They shook hands and nodded to each other. An understanding and a promise was made and secured.

'And to you, Sholto.'

Jock waved Sholto off as he drove away in his car. He paused for a moment outside the bar restaurant, feeling that Sholto, his sons and Cairn would be back, and everyone would be better off for leaving grudges where they belonged — in the past.

The next morning an insistent knock sounded on the front door of the dress shop.

Eila padded through in her fluffy slippers and jim–jams. Her hair was in a messy ponytail. She tried and failed to straighten it up.

Gordon stood outside, wearing his swimming trunks, towel clutched in one hand.

Her heart reacted seeing his strong, lean build through the window.

She opened the door, not feeling the need to tidy herself up. He'd seen her at her best, so now he'd have to see her tumbled and tousled with a wonky ponytail and face scrubbed free of makeup.

'Come on, sleepyhead, we're going swimming.'

She smiled, and hurried away to put her swimsuit on.

Gordon led them to the calm, deep blue–grey sea. They had the shore all to themselves.

Eila gave up on her ponytail, shaking her hair down around her shoulders.

The sand beneath her feet was quite warm, but the water looked cold.

Gordon didn't hesitate and waded in. He held out his hand to her. 'Come on, take the plunge.'

Eila put her hands on her hips in mock defiance. 'I'm working up to it. I'm still half sleeping.'

Gordon sank down until the water was lapping around his shoulders. 'Feels tepid to me,' he lied.

Eila squinted at him. 'I'm getting to know all your looks. I think you're fibbing.'

Gordon relaxed back and floated on the surface, sucking up the cold of the water, but becoming accustomed to it. He felt that Eila was becoming accustomed to him, and planned to take their friendship to the next level. He sensed the time was right.

Eila dipped a toe in the water. 'It's not as warm as it was a few days ago.' The summer was fast drawing to a close.

He stood up, and she felt her stomach tense seeing the taut muscles on his torso and the way the water trickled down over his shoulders and arms. It emphasised his strong, lithe build.

'You swim and I'll paddle around, get acclimatised.' She got ready to run. She'd seen that mischievous look on his face before. The last time she'd ended up with buttercream on the end of her nose.

Gordon walked out of the sea, picked her up before she could run, and carried her into the water until he was waist deep.

She clutched on to his shoulders, feeling the strength of his muscles beneath her fingers.

'No, Gordon, no!' she laughed and yelled.

Gordon pretended he was going to throw her in, lifting her with ease, swinging her over the water and then walked back out and placed her safely on the sand.

She slapped him playfully and laughed.

Eila was so busy laughing she didn't hear the sleek silver car pull up on the esplanade.

Cairn stepped out, dressed in a classy suit, and stood watching her with Gordon. He heard the sound of her laughter ringing clear in the fresh air. Her happiness meant everything to him. He sighed heavily, and reluctantly admitted to himself that Eila was happy with Gordon. It was obvious from watching them that they were a lovely, happy couple.

Cairn had driven from Edinburgh before the dawn, unable to sleep, wanting to talk to her, to explain why he'd left without saying goodbye. He wanted to assure her that he was coming back with Sholto and the others.

When he'd walked away from the tea shop that night before driving off to Edinburgh, he thought he'd be back soon and that maybe...maybe he would let his feelings for her be known. But bad timing, circumstances and someone better suited to her, had all conspired against him. He loved her, but he knew she'd forge a life with Gordon.

If their romance fizzled out, he'd be there sometime in the future. Eila had brought out the best in him, and he felt the benefit of having known her, having felt his heart melt, a rare experience, but in business had no place in his world. He'd secured the business deal with the film company and their recent requirements.

He should've been in Edinburgh working on the designs this morning with Sholto, Hamish and Fraser, but he needed to see Eila, to explain, to say goodbye, and yet...he knew what he needed to do.

Cairn took one last longing look at Eila enjoying herself in the sea with Gordon...

Eila laughed as Gordon lifted her up in the shallows and swung her around. She held on tight and nuzzled into his shoulder, determined not to let go, to prevent herself being thrown in.

But Gordon paused and smiled at her, then said, 'I love you, Eila.' He smiled again, pulled her close and kissed her, warm and tender at first and then with passion.

She smiled, breathless with excitement. 'I love you too, Gordon.'

Then for a moment, a feeling shot through her — a sense of something, someone...

Eila glanced up to the esplanade, but there was no one, only the sound of a car driving off into the distance.

Shrugging off the feeling, she smiled warmly at Gordon and kissed him again and again, before they both dived into the water and swam together in the sea.

End

About the Author:

De-ann Black is a bestselling author, scriptwriter and former newspaper journalist. She has over 70 books published. Romance, crime thrillers, espionage novels, action adventure. And children's books (non-fiction rocket science books and children's fiction). She became an Amazon All-Star author in 2014 and 2015.

She previously worked as a full-time newspaper journalist for several years. She had her own weekly columns in the press. This included being a motoring correspondent where she got to test drive cars every week for the press for three years.

Before being asked to work for the press, De-ann worked in magazine editorial writing everything from fashion features to social news. She was the marketing editor of a glossy magazine. She is also a professional artist and illustrator. Fabric design, dressmaking, sewing, knitting and fashion are part of her work.

Additionally, De-ann has always been interested in fitness, and was a fitness and bodybuilding champion, 100 metre runner and mountaineer. As a former N.A.B.B.A. Miss Scotland, she had a weekly fitness show on the radio that ran for over three years.

De-ann trained in Shukokai karate, boxing, kickboxing, Dayan Qigong and Jiu Jitsu. She is currently based in Scotland.

Her colouring books and embroidery design books are available in paperback. These include Floral Nature Embroidery Designs and Scottish Garden Embroidery Designs.

Find out more at: www.de-annblack.com

Printed in Great Britain
by Amazon